WONDERLAND

WONDERLAND

ROB BROWATZKE

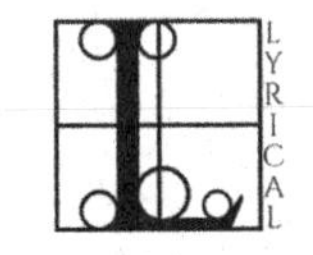

LYRICAL PRESS
Kensington Publishing Corp.
www.kensingtonbooks.com

LYRICAL PRESS BOOKS are published by

Kensington Publishing Corp.
119 West 40th Street
New York, NY 10018

All Kensington titles, imprints, and distributed lines are available at special quantity discounts for bulk purchases for sales promotion, premiums, fund-raising, educational, or institutional use.

Special book excerpts or customized printings can also be created to fit specific needs. For details, write or phone the office of the Kensington Special Sales Manager: Kensington Publishing Corp., 119 West 40th Street, New York, NY 10018. Attn. Special Sales Department. Phone: 1-800-221-2647.

Lyrical and the L logo Reg. U.S. Pat. & TM Off.

First Electronic Edition: February 2015
eISBN-13: 978-1-60183-368-6
eISBN-10: 1-60183-386-7

First Print Edition: February 2015
ISBN-13: 978-1-60183-369-3
ISBN-10: 1-60183-369-5

Printed in the United States of America

To Lewis Carroll, for his curiouser and curiouser story that
has ignited the imaginations of so many.
To all the boys down all the rabbit holes.

Chapter 1

I looked around the club and couldn't believe no one seemed to care. The party was still going on! In the booth, the Hatter was on the decks, spinning away, without a worry in the world, and below him, on the dance floor, it was a sea of bodies, shirtless, glittered, glistening. Strobes flashed and lasers wove among the crowd, and heads were thrown back, hands in the air, in ecstasy. On Ecstasy, maybe. Who knew? Sure enough, the Caterpillar was at his table, and people visited him briefly, their money for his drugs, and then they were off to the bathroom, to snort, to drop, to bump whatever he'd sold them.

The air vibrated. It was the bass pounding off the dance floor, it was a hundred conversations being yelled out over the din. Here, the twins, in their matching tanks, eyes closed, muscles bulging, as they gyrated together in a cage. There, a flock of mindless twinks, fluttering about in the drama of the moment. Didn't they know? Didn't they care?

I sipped my gin and cran, and shook my head. I wanted to scream! Wanted to grab some passing boy and shake him till he understood. Maybe he'd only mattered to me. Maybe I was the only one who really loved him. Maybe to everyone else, he'd just been a face in the crowd, just one nameless pretty boy among all the other nameless pretty boys.

From the first moment I laid eyes on him though, getting into his white VW Rabbit, he had been so much more to me than just some nameless pretty boy. Sure, right then, he'd just been nameless and pretty, but for the brief second his gaze met mine across the parking lot, we connected. In those few seconds, I imagined a hundred scenarios, and in all of them, we ended up with a white-picket fence, happy-ever-after in Suburbia, away from this sea of smooth bodies, fast beats, and hard drugs.

Away from Wonderland.

But no, now he was gone, and the party was still going, and I was still sitting here, on my perch at the bar, where I sat night in and night out, watching the freak-show train wreck I called my life. And no one in this club could give a shit. Give a bump maybe, or get shittered, but actually care? Actually reach out and genuinely connect with another human being?

Unlikely.

The Hatter spun, and the Caterpillar sold, and the people danced, and I sat there, staring at my ice cubes, thinking it was time to go home, knowing I would order one more. It was a Friday night, and that's what I did. What we all did. We left our real world, our nine-to-fives, our condos in the sky, and we came down here, under the traffic, to a dirty little hole that lit up with beautiful lights, and even more beautiful people.

"Another?"

It was Brandon, beautiful and blond, all abs to the front, all amazing ass to the rear, and he was leaning across the bar. His eyes were blue, and my drink was empty.

"Sure." His fingers brushed the back of my hand as he took away my empty, replaced it with another.

"On me," he said, and he was back to the lineup. I watched him for a while, doing the graceful dance of the bartender. He spun about, pouring shots, cracking beers, dispensing drinks and flirts and seven-dollar ounces of happiness.

I twirled the drink around in my hands. I really had had enough, and I knew I should go, but I hoped he'd come. Still. Even though the Hatter had already announced last call for the first time. Even though the last thing Steven had said to me was that he never wanted to see me again. He couldn't have meant it though. It was the heat of the moment and when he calmed down, when we both calmed down, we'd work it out. He'd come down those stairs, and through the crowd, and he'd take me by the hand and lead me to the dance floor, and with our bodies pressed together, we would kiss under the strobe, like we did that first night, and everything would be the way it was.

"You have five minutes left until last call," the Hatter counted down on the mic, and Kesha mixed with One Direction, and the twinks squealed and the dance floor, already full, bulged with more people, one big writhing mass of beautiful, tragic homos. And not one of them knew or cared that he was gone, and it was over, and my drink was empty again.

"Brandon!" I yelled as he spun past me, dropping drinks down at the other end of the bar.

"Another?"

"Make it two," I said, and slid a twenty toward him. He dropped off the drinks and my change, and I took the drinks, left the change. It was just money. And his ass was easily worth the tip.

I pushed back my stool, lurched to my feet, drink in each hand, and fought my way through the crowd. Eyes went up and down me, in that judging homo way. My eyes went up and down the people I passed, just as judging. I wove my way through fat straight girls and their skinny gay best friends, past the plaid-wearing lesbians playing pool in the corner, my eyes on the Caterpillar. I knew I shouldn't. I knew Steven wouldn't like it.

But he hadn't come. And if all these people didn't care, why should I?

"Alex!" I heard my name as an arm wrapped around my waist. An arm attached to the gleaming torso of one of the twins. He pulled me into him, and I lifted my drinks over his shoulders as we hugged, as we kissed each other's cheeks. "How's your night?"

"It's a night," I said, sipping my drink, my eyes darting past whichever twin this was to the table in the corner, where the Caterpillar watched and waited. "Yours?"

"Where's Steven?"

There it was. His name. Hearing it made my chest tighten. "He didn't come out tonight."

"Too bad! Come dance with us!" He went to take me by the hand as his look-alike came up and grabbed me by the other. I felt my drink spill down my arm.

"No, I was just headed home. I—"

"One dance?" Two matching smiles, four matching dimples, four sparkling green eyes, so much muscle. How could I say no? And with Steven not here, why should I say no?

And then we were on the dance floor, hands in the air, and I had one in front of me, grinding back into my crotch, and one behind me, grinding into my butt, and all around me, people danced and laughed and drank, and the lights were bright, and the music was wordless and fast, and faster and faster we danced, and I finished my drinks and threw back my head, and let myself get lost in the moment.

Steven hadn't come. I had waited and waited and waited, and he hadn't come. He had made his choice. The twin behind me was kissing my neck. I tilted my head back and met his lips with mine. He tasted like berries.

I twisted around so we were facing each other. Behind me, the other one lifted up my shirt, and I let him take it off. His lips were on my shoulders, and I paused briefly, thinking how I must look between their tanned and toned bodies. But then the one behind me slid a hand into my pants and I stopped thinking. And we danced and we kissed, sweat and skin and sweet sweet sin.

In the mirror that ran along the dance floor, I saw us, and what a sight we were, the three of us, three among the many, and it was wonderful and it was beautiful and it was wrong. It wasn't Steven. And there, at the end of the mirror, I could see the Caterpillar's reflection, as he sat there, beer in hand, and watched and waited.

Waited for me?

I squirmed out from between the twins, and their hands followed mine until the crowd separated us, and I looked back at them. Their hands had found each other, and they were kissing, and people watched as they danced, because the twins were beautiful and shirtless and gleaming, looking enough like actual brothers to be forbidden, taboo, exciting. I wound my way across the floor and up the stairs, and sat down across from the Caterpillar.

He smiled at me, raised his beer in salute. I raised an eyebrow in question, and I could feel the desperation on my face. It was late. What if he was out? He nodded, and I could feel the relief and the guilt and the excitement all mingle inside me. I slid my hand across the table, money hidden in my palm. He shook my hand, and I could feel the money disappear, feel the familiar little plastic Baggie.

Away from the Caterpillar I went, and back through the throng, now even more frenzied as the Hatter announced, "Last song of the night." People were flooding onto the dance floor, and I was going against the stream, headed to the bathroom, where the strobes and lasers and swirling color went away, in an ugly fluorescent glare. I locked the stall behind me, ignoring the water all over the floor, the clumped toilet paper, the unflushed bowl.

I held up the Baggie, flicked it to loosen it, opened it up. I dipped in my key, scooped out some powder, and inhaled. My body tensed and then loosened. I was floating on fire.

Tucking the Baggie into my jeans, I checked my reflection in the mirror, looking for any telltale signs of drug use. Finding none, and not really caring either way, I went back out in the club, where everything seemed more real now. The music was just a little clearer, the lights were just a tad brighter. The twins were still lip-locked on the dance floor. I fought my way toward them, and reached them just as the song faded away into the silence of a hundred conversations, laughter and shrieks and disjointed words.

I was high and alive, and I had a twin on each side, and as the three of us found our way out of Wonderland and into the world above, I looked around the club one last time, and right then, I didn't care either.

Chapter 2

I woke up the morning after the night before sandwiched between the twins. It was morning breath and morning wood, and the pounding of too many gin and crans. The light was streaming through the window, and that definitely didn't help. Damn Brandon and his cute ass! Damn Caterpillar and his good blow! Damn Steven and his stubborn pride!

That wasn't the way the night had been supposed to go.

I lay there, holding my palms against my forehead, willing the hangover to go away. The twin on my right stirred, and when the sheet fell away from his belly, revealing a sun around his belly button, hard abs, and a harder dick, I grimaced. What had I done?

Colton opened his eyes. "Morning," he said, reaching out to rub my cheek.

"Morning."

"How are you feeling?"

"Been better."

"You were insatiable. Steven's a lucky guy."

"Thanks. Look, last night . . . it was a mistake. Steven can't ever know."

"No worries." He pulled me into him, kissing me. I let him kiss me before I pulled back.

"I can't." I wanted to, oh how I wanted to! Colton was beautiful, Colton was there. Steven wasn't. "I can't," I repeated, less insistent. Behind me, I felt Jesse wake up, felt him pressing into me, felt his breath on my ear.

"You can," Jesse whispered. Both their heads went down. I exhaled deeply. Not the way it had been supposed to go at all. But they were here, and they were beautiful, and if that wasn't a good excuse, it was excuse enough.

When we were done, we showered, all together, the relaxed and awkward cleansing that happens after a good romp. I watched them as I got dressed and they toweled each other off. They were so comfortable with each other, the ease that only comes after years of being together. Steven and I had never had that ease. Maybe in time we would have. He hadn't been willing to give us the time. Hadn't been willing to forgive me for the mistake I'd made.

"Shall we brunch?" Colton asked. His arms wrapped around Jesse, and they were both looking at me, all smiles and dimples. *That's how I got here,* I thought, *those damn dimples.* But I nodded. I was hungry, and maybe food would be a balm to my guilty conscience.

Why should I be guilty though? Hadn't Steven said we were done? Why shouldn't I dance and fuck and be free? What was I supposed to do? Light the candles, turn up the power ballads, and drown my sorrows in a bottle of wine? I wasn't nineteen anymore.

Stupid like a nineteen-year-old, though, I thought as I felt the Baggie through my jeans, felt the hard box in my pocket. What had I been thinking? Did I really think that some grandiose gesture was going to make everything okay? I wondered if I could get the money back for the ring; I knew I couldn't for the drugs. You can never put the powder back into the Baggie.

"Yes, let's brunch." They wrapped their arms around my shoulders, and off we went.

Brunch at the Duchess was Saturday tradition. Steven and I had gone every week. As Jesse and Colton and I were shown to our table, we nodded greetings to people we knew, people we'd seen at the club the night before. Occasionally, one would get up to greet us with a kiss. Gays and their brunches! Cheapest mimosas and the best hollandaise in the city though, and that's what I ordered. Steven would have had an omelet; I always ordered my eggs Benedict.

I remembered the first time Steven and I had gone for brunch there. It was the morning after our first night together. I was glowing. We talked, about everything, about nothing. And then we'd gone for a walk in the river valley, sipping on lattes we had picked up at one of the many Starbucks in the gayborhood. The walk led to lunch, which led to dinner, and before either of us knew it, we had spent the weekend together, and I'd known I loved him.

"Alex! Colton! Jesse!" We turned our heads, nearly as one, at the approach of Brandon, whose lean lanky beauty was single-handedly responsible for my hangover (albeit, the mimosa in my hand was rapidly easing the headache). On Brandon's arm was a pretty boy I didn't know, one who Brandon introduced as Allan.

"Flavor of the week," Jesse whispered to me, even as Colton invited them to join us. Allan had blue-gray eyes that peered out from behind black glasses. Blond hair poked out from under a backward blue ball cap, and his hand never let get of Brandon's.

"Hope you guys had fun at the club last night," Brandon said. "And you bitches better be out tonight for my birthday. I will make sure you're guest-listed."

"We'll be there," Colton said, and Jesse nodded.

"What about you, Alex?" Brandon said, and he flashed me that irresistible smile.

I had a ring in my pocket, and no one's hand to put it on. "Yes, I'll be there."

Our food came, and Brandon entertained us with stories from the night before, part fabulous, part tragic, all gossip. Allan hung on his every word, poor kid. Brandon went through fresh-faced twinklets like I went through gin and crans. Steven and I used to laugh about it. We couldn't keep them straight, the Shanes and Shawns and Austins.

"Earth to Alex."

"Sorry?"

"I was asking you where Steven was last night."

"I . . . I don't know. We . . . had a fight."

That was the understatement of the year. I'd never seen Steven so angry. I should've known he would be. He hated drugs. That was one of the first things he'd told me, on our river valley walk, that first Saturday, after our first Friday. Months ago, when everything was new, and we had nothing ahead but possibility.

Jesse and Colton were laughing at the inane story Brandon was telling, Allan gazing up at him with undisguised adoration. I couldn't do it, couldn't be around all the happy. Not to mention the guilt every time I looked at one of the twins. I needed to find Steven and throw myself at his feet and beg forgiveness.

I pushed my chair back. "I need to go, guys." I dropped some money on the table.

"See you tonight?" Jesse asked.

"Yah, I'll be there."

"You better, bee-yotch," Brandon said, and blew me a kiss.

I left the Duchess and headed home. I checked my phone and there were no missed calls, no unanswered texts. I dialed Steven's number. It went straight to voice mail, and his voice mail was full. He had never been good with his phone, definitely didn't live on it like I did. He hadn't tweeted, he hadn't Facebooked. Oh the wonders of social media! Never before had it been so easy to keep tabs on a missing boyfriend.

Well, ex-boyfriend. He had said we were over, and a night of drugs and threeways surely sealed that deal. Especially if he ever found out. Which he would. Keeping secrets in this little gayborhood was impossible. Big city, but a small town. Everyone knew everyone's business, and it was just a matter of time before Steven found out what had happened.

The only thing to do was man up and tell him first.

I was about to reach my building but did an about-face and headed toward Steven's house. Summer was definitely over. Leaves were falling from the trees. The streets were lined with them. Gold and brown and red, they were clogging the sewer grates. I reached into my pocket, felt the ring box, pulled out the Baggie, and shoved it through the leaves into the sewer.

That had been even dumber than going home with the twins, but it had seemed like a good idea at the time, in the gin-induced fog. Steven didn't need to know about that, either. If he forgave me for the threeway, that would be a miracle. He sure wouldn't forgive me for visiting the Caterpillar. Not twice.

I turned onto his street. There was his house. His car was outside, that cute little Volkswagen he'd been driving the first time I saw him. Had it only been six months? The leaves were just starting to come back after the long winter when we met. Now they were falling. What a summer it had been though. The summer of me and Steven.

I kept walking past. I couldn't face him. Not yet.

Chapter 3

It was a Friday. I'd finished work at the bank, and had stopped to grab some groceries. I'd unloaded them from my cart and was just closing my trunk when I saw him. One row over and a few spaces down, he was standing there, his bags on the roof of his white Rabbit. He was taller than me, probably six two, and looked like he worked out. His dress shirt was tight across his chest, his tie loosened just right. He looked right at me and smiled. White teeth and a bum chin.

I had never seen anyone so handsome.

Oh sure, I'd seen lots of gorgeous men, but sometimes their beauty just masked the emptiness within. This guy, he carried himself with confidence, not just ego. He was sharply dressed, but not superficially so. He was well rounded, grounded, intelligent, and funny. I could tell. Two seconds of eye contact and I knew all I needed to know.

And he was getting into his car and I'd never see him again.

That couldn't happen!

As he got into his car, I got into mine, and as he pulled out, I did the same. This was crazy. Was I actually going to follow a guy home from the Safeway? As I followed him into traffic, I realized that was exactly what I was going to do.

Traffic was slow and tight as we headed downtown, and I could keep him in sight easily. I stayed a few cars behind him. In my mind,

I was already picturing our wedding, me and this tall, dark, and handsome stranger whom I was stalking across the bridge. It was romantic, what I was doing, right? Love, first sight, right? I had convinced myself, and signaled to change lanes. I would pull up next to him, and he'd yell out his number at me, and that would be that.

But as I pulled left, he went right.

"Shit!" I swore, and swerved back over. A car honked, and slammed on its brakes. I waved at the driver, who was flipping me off, and swerved into the far right lane. Where was he? I scanned the traffic ahead for the white Rabbit. There it was, and I exited the road, following him.

Completely crazy.

He was stopped at a red light. I pulled into the lane next to him and looked over. He wasn't looking back. Should I honk? *No, that would be too much,* I thought, not that this whole thing wasn't completely ridiculous anyway. We pulled out from the light when it went green. As we did, he glanced my way, and we had eye contact again! And there it was, that smile. I wanted to wave, but in the split second I had to decide, he turned right.

I tried to get over, but couldn't. Cars cut me off, and by the time I got over, I was two blocks past where he'd turned. I backtracked. The street he had turned onto was all cute little houses, all identical. The Rabbit was parked but he was nowhere to be seen! Which house was his? Damn! I pulled to the curb in front of his car. What could I do? Knock on doors at random?

Hi, I just spent half an hour following you through the city, but I'm not crazy. Honest.

No. That wouldn't work. I reached over to my glove box, took out a pen and paper. I could leave a note on his windshield, but what would I say? This wasn't how it was supposed to be. He was supposed to be standing outside waiting for me. No. A note wouldn't work either.

"You're being ridiculous, Alex," I said out loud. "Just go home." I was right, like usual. The whole thing was just a ludicrous idea in the first place. People don't see people in a parking lot and then spend the rest of their lives together. That didn't happen. I backed up to pull away . . . backed up right into his car.

"Fuck!" I said, slamming my fists on the steering wheel and accidentally honking my own horn. And then I saw him, coming out of his house across the street. I turned off my engine and got out of my car.

"What the hell, dude?" he said.

"Sorry, sorry, my bad." He was even hotter up close, and with his jacket off, I could make out the bulge of a well-defined bicep through his shirt.

He paused and looked at me. "Didn't I just see you at Safeway?" he asked.

"Yeah, I think so!"

We looked at the cars, and luckily neither was damaged. Or not luckily. If I'd hit it a little harder, I'd have had to give him my phone number for insurance purposes, but with no damage, I would just leave and he'd be out of my life unless . . .

"Well, I guess there's no damage, so—"

"Wannagofordinner?" I interrupted him.

"Sorry?"

"Would you like to go for dinner?"

He raised an eyebrow, looked me up and down, and smiled. "Well, I better drive though, I think."

"Probably a good idea." My face was hot as I extended my hand. "I'm Alex."

His hand was smooth and his handshake firm. "Hi. I'm Steven."

He took me to a cute little Italian place a few blocks down, and after we'd ordered some wine, he asked me, "So do you live around here then?"

"Well, about a dozen blocks or so."

"Visiting?"

"Well, actually, no." The waiter came back with the wine, and as he poured us both a glass, I took Steven in with my eyes. Once I finished confessing that I had followed him from the grocery store like a crazy person, I was sure he would get up and leave me there to finish the wine myself. I sipped the wine. It had quite a lovely taste, so at least he wasn't about to leave me with a cheap bottle. "The truth is," I continued, taking a deep breath (and another sip), "I kinda followed you."

"You did what?" Steven paused mid-drink.

I laughed nervously. "It's completely insane, I know, but I saw you in the parking lot, and just thought, go for it."

"You backed into my car just to get to meet me?"

"No, that part was accidental."

"You're a mental case."

"A bit." I took another sip. "Are you staying?"

"Do you see me leaving?"

"It's actually your fault," I said, taking his continued presence as a sign to forge ahead.

"How so?"

"You're far too good-looking to smile at strangers in parking lots."

"I don't expect them to follow me home."

"I was a stray cat in a previous life."

"Then I should be careful what I feed you."

"Well, it *is* a good wine."

"Try the pumpkin ravioli."

"Sounds delicious. I might not leave."

"I might not ask you to," he said, and he reached across the table and touched my hand. There was that smile again. "That being said, though, you're completely insane."

"I'm well aware, but in this case, it looks like it worked out."

"So far."

"Yes, so far."

The waiter came back up to the table. "Do you see anything you like?"

"I think I do," Steven said, and the smile as he looked at me told me he didn't mean the pumpkin ravioli.

Chapter 4

I met Jesse and Colton outside the club for Brandon's birthday bash. They were in matching black tanks, which had to be cold. There was a definite hint of winter in the air.

"Alex!" they said as one, hugging me. They were both too pretty for my own good. "Still no Steven?"

He hadn't called. He hadn't replied to a text. His car was still outside his house, or at least had been when I was walking to the club. "No."

"What was the fight about?" Colton asked.

How to sum it up? Dreading turning thirty, I'd decided to pop the question, causing me to panic and buy drugs, which Steven then found and blew up about? "It doesn't matter," I said. "Let's get a drink."

Brandon had gone all out for his party, and greeted us at the bottom of the stairs. Shirtless, bow-tied, all abs and ass, he stood there, Allan on his arm. Allan was already sporting a white ring on his nose. Kids today and their K! The club itself was all black light, glowing green and orange and yellow, and the Hatter was above us, spinning some deep house. Jesse and Colton pulled off their shirts in one synchronized fluid motion.

"We're dancing," they said, kissing Brandon, kissing me, and then they were off, into the crowd, two gods among so many gods.

"Thanks for coming," Brandon said, kissing me again.

"I wouldn't have missed it for the world. Can I get you a drink?"

"Vodka seven, thanks."

"Allan?" I offered.

"I'm good, thanks."

I slid through the crowd to the bar, got the drinks, delivered Brandon his, and then found my normal stool, the corner of the bar, facing the dance floor, where I could watch the people come in, watch them drink and dance and love and leave. I sipped my gin and cran and looked around, scanning the crowd for Steven.

The Caterpillar came toward me, a smile on his face. "Alex!" he said. "How goes your night?"

"Going well," I said, trying to be as cold as possible.

He leaned in close. "Going to need anything tonight?"

"Not tonight. Sorry, I'm done."

He smirked. He'd heard that before, I'm sure, from so many people. "I'm around if you change your mind."

He slinked off into the crowd. His suit was glowing. Everyone was glowing. I looked down at my outfit, which was white enough to give me a glow of my own. Just another random glow Saturday in Wonderland.

There was a pause in the music and the dance floor cleared as a pumping overture came on. I perked up, ordered another drink, and watched as the resident drag queen came onto the stage, her dark hair piled high on her head, her dress shimmering and red. As the music started, she was joined by Brandon, by Allan, by a couple other nameless pretty boys, and as her backup dancers bounced and thrust with choreographed fluidity, the Queen of Hearts performed.

I watched, enraptured as always. She was grace and elegance and perfection. Small wonder she was the only resident queen in the club. Who else did they need? She owned the room and everyone in it, from tweaked-out club kid to gym bunny to leather daddy. I watched, and drank, and when the song was over, I clapped and cheered as much as the rest. And then she was gone.

"What did you think?" Brandon asked, throwing his arm around me. He was slick with sweat, and I could feel his abs flex against my arm with every panted breath.

"It was great! She always is," I said.

"I know she is. What did you think of me?"

"Oh, well, you were great too."

"We rehearsed all afternoon." He leaned into me closer. "Did you think it was hot?"

Curious, I thought, he'd never hit on me before. "Very hot," I said, and turned into his face. Our lips were inches apart.

"There you are!" Allan squealed, grabbing Brandon by the shoulder. "Let's go for a bump."

Brandon rolled his eyes and smirked at me. Without looking away, he reached into his pocket and pulled out his bumper bottle. "Here, go, I'm good." Allan glared at me, but took the bottle and ran off to the bathroom.

"So Alex," Brandon said, "what's up with you and Steven?"

"We had a fight," I said. "It will blow over, I hope. He was pretty mad."

"What about?"

"Drugs."

"I didn't think you partied."

"I don't really. Well, it was a bad week. It was dumb."

"Oh, I'm not one to judge." His hand was on my thigh. I was very aware of his hand on my thigh. "Maybe we should party together sometime."

"I'm flattered but I really want to work things out with Steven. And what about Allan?"

"What about Allan? You don't think he's cute?"

"He's adorable, Brandon. All your boys are."

"Maybe you can party with both of us. I mean, I hear you're a pretty good third."

Damn Jesse and Colton! "That was a mistake too."

"Well, if you want to make another mistake this weekend, it *is* my birthday," he said, and his hand slid up my thigh to my crotch. I couldn't help but grunt as he squeezed. He squeezed hard, but I was suddenly harder.

Allan was back, and dragging him away. Brandon looked back at me and winked, and then his abs disappeared into the crowd. I shifted on my stool, ordered another drink. As the bartender, some new ginger cub called Tom or Todd, brought it to me, I looked across to the dance floor, where Brandon and Allan flailed about to the Hatter's hard house, where Jesse and Colton claimed their cage.

I could see where this night was going to go. And before it went there, I decided it was best to leave. I tipped back my last drink, and lost myself in the crowd, hoping none of my friends saw me as I snuck up and out. Luckily none did, and when I was out in the fresh night air, away from the throbbing bass and equally throbbing temptations of hot men, I thought again of Steven.

Chapter 5

After we finished dinner, Steven drove me back to my car. The sun was starting to go down. As I unlocked my car door, he said, "I'm glad you backed into me." Smiling, I turned around. He was right behind me. And then he was kissing me, and I was kissing him. My keys fell to the ground.

"Want to go dancing?" he asked.

I wasn't a big bar person. When I'd first come out, of course, it was the bar every night, but that had been years before, and then I'd been in a relationship for six years, rarely going out. After that, when Aaron and I broke up, I turned my focus to work and hadn't set foot in a dance club in two years.

"Absolutely," I replied.

"Okay, I just want to change." Steven took me by the hand and led me into his house. It was tidier than my condo, that's for sure, and had a long aquarium running along the wall between the living room and the kitchen. "Make yourself at home," he said. "I'll be right out."

I looked at his fish, looked at some pictures on the wall. He was responsible, traveled. "Alex!" he called from down the hall. "Did you want to change? I probably have something that would fit."

I looked down at my work clothes, and no, they weren't really suitable for a night out on the town. I was smaller than Steven, but not by enough that something he had wouldn't fit. "Sure." I walked down the hall toward his bedroom. He was standing there, shirt off, his chest hair perfectly trimmed over his sculpted pecs, so beautiful, holding first one, then another shirt up to his reflection in the mirror.

"Nice," I said.

"This shirt?"

"That everything." I leered at him.

He laughed. I loved his laugh, it was rich and deep. "Here, try this on." He tossed me a shirt.

As I took mine off, he whistled appreciatively. I felt myself blush. As I pulled his shirt over my head, I felt his hands on my chest. My body broke into goose bumps. He pulled the shirt down and kissed me again. I kissed him back, harder this time, and he took a step back, pulling me with him, falling onto the bed, pulling me down on top of him.

It was hot! I hadn't been with anyone in the two years since Aaron and I had split. Well, that's not true. There was that guy from Pride the year before, but it barely counted. It was quick and meaningless and didn't have anywhere near the passion that those first kisses with Steven did. Steven rolled onto me, raised my hands above my head, lifted his face away from mine. I strained upward, wanting his lips on mine again. He pulled away, laughing again.

"Later," he said. He got up, finished dressing. I lay there, panting. "Shall we?" he said, offering me his hand.

Instead of letting him pull me up, I pulled him down. He laughed and we kissed again. I could feel him pressing into me. I rolled on top. His hands went up my shirt, his thumbs teasing my nipples. I rolled off him and stood up.

"Okay, let's go." I could play that game too.

The club he was taking me to was called Wonderland, and it was only a few blocks away from his house. As we walked down the street, he took my hand in his. Now, I wasn't normally big on PDAs, but as he wrapped his fingers in between mine, it felt quite natural. I didn't pull away. After all, I'd backed into this guy's car. What was a little hand-holding?

"Do you go out often?" I asked him.

Steven shrugged. "It's close." He paused. "It's a nice way to unwind after a hard week at work."

I could think of several ways I'd rather help him unwind, but I knew that it would happen eventually. The sexual tension between us was palpable, and I couldn't wait to get my mouth back onto his hot body. Drinks and dancing were just prolonging the inevitable, and would only make it hotter. I wondered, not for the first time, if he was a top or a bottom. I glanced down at his butt as he walked—it was definitely fuckable. But I'd also felt him pressing into me, and could definitely see him actually *in* me. Time would tell. . . .

My thoughts stopped abruptly as we turned the corner and were met by a giant flower. Well, a shirtless muscle man, fake leaves around his waist and head. "Steven!" he said, hugging Steven with wrists equally leaf-clad. He was hot. I'd never wished I was a bumblebee before.

"Jesse!" Steven greeted. "This is Alex."

"Nice to meet you." His handshake was firm, his smile broad. "You're probably wondering about the outfit."

"A bit," I said, even as Steven said, "It's the garden party already?"

"Yessir! Colton's at the other end of the block. He's a rose."

"That he is," Steven said. "And doesn't he smell sweet?"

"Find your own flower!" Jesse said, winking at me. He reached into the waistband of his green undies, and pulled out a couple cards. "VIP passes for the night. They're good for no cover and a free drink."

"Thanks, doll," Steven said, taking the cards and smiling at me. "This is Alex's first time."

"Oooh! Well, Alex, any friend of Steven's . . ." He hugged me, then Steven, taking care not to squash his petals. "Have a good time, guys!"

I'd been in many gay bars over the years but nothing quite prepared me for the sight inside. Giant flowers towered overhead, some in fabric, some in paint, all glowed, all glittered. The floorboards were hidden with fake rosebushes, the stairwell down into the club was covered in red gravel. As we turned off the stairs, the lights hit my eyes, colored shapes and laser lines, a dozen disco balls tossing out hundreds of swirling spots of light, and all of it was set to a soundtrack of pulsating house music, being spun by a DJ in a giant purple hat.

And the men! If I hadn't only had eyes for Steven, I'd have hurt my neck straining it about. Smooth and hard bodies were everywhere, some muscled, some slender, all glistening. It was like walking onto a movie set—not like the gay club back home, that's for sure.

Steven looked at me. "Welcome to Wonderland," he said, and he kissed my cheek.

"Wow!" I yelled over the music. "This place is crazy!"

"It's not always this over the top, but they go all out for their theme parties. Drink?"

"Sure!" He pulled me by my hand through the crowd, to a bar decorated to look like a hedge maze, and from the center of the maze, bartenders served drinks with speed and smiles. The one Steven led us to was ripped and blond, and when he leaned down to get Steven a beer, his ass was to die for.

We traded in our VIP cards for our drinks, then Steven dragged me to the dance floor, and pulled me in tight to him. "What do you think?"

"It's wonderful!"

"So are you." He kissed me, and then no matter how bedazzled the club or how beautiful the men, I forgot everything else. It was just that kiss, flooding me with music and energy.

"I'm glad I backed into you," I told him, as we pulled apart.

He threw back his head and laughed. "Crazy guy. Let's dance!"

Chapter 6

The lights were on at Steven's house, the car was still outside. I glanced at my phone—nothing. I debated knocking. No, it was best not. How things had changed from the day I barely thought twice about following him home from a grocery store.

That really had been crazy, and I probably would never have done it if it hadn't been for the fact that I was completely over Aaron, and really ready to get back on the horse. I'd given up my condo, my city, my whole life, to get away from the rut that was Aaron, and after two years in a new city and only one Grindr hookup on Pride, I leapt at the connection I'd thought I felt.

Aaron. I never thought about him. We'd been together for six years. And if it wasn't ever great, it wasn't ever bad. It just . . . was. We were comfortable with each other. By the end, maybe too comfortable. Not like pooping-with-the-door-open comfortable, don't get me wrong. My parents did that, and it was gross. But we had no surprises anymore. No passion.

So I'd left. And there hadn't even been a big teary scene. We sold the condo, split the money, and he found a new place while I got transferred to the big city and got myself my little apartment. And I dove into work, wanting to get stabilized.

Stabilized to the point where I backed into some hot guy's car, and then proceeded to fall madly in love with him.

Because don't get me wrong. The threeway and drugs aside, I did love Steven. It was just . . . thirty was looming ahead of me, and I panicked. Should six months of an amazing relationship get thrown away for one night of a bad decision? Okay, two nights.

At least I'd bailed tonight before I made it three. Brandon had never hit on me before. What had been up with that?

A silhouette moved in Steven's house. Why was I standing out here watching? He was home. I should just go knock and get it over with. If I confessed and apologized, he'd forgive me, and then things would get back to normal, not this bizarro world we'd lived in the past two days.

I crossed the street toward his house, past his Rabbit.

There were two silhouettes.

Steven wasn't alone.

I about-faced and crossed back over. I couldn't even be mad seeing as I'd spent the night with the twins. And who knew if it was a trick anyway? It could just be a friend. Their shadows came together. Okay, not just a friend. But how could I be mad at him for doing what I'd already done? Two wrongs made a right, in this case, right?

I walked away, not daring to look back. I decided I would call in the morning, would let him have his night of indiscretion too. Then we were even. Steven.

Chapter 7

Sunday brunch at the Duchess was basically a repeat of Saturday brunch at the Duchess, just with more mimosas. I was exhausted. Every time I'd closed my eyes, I'd pictured Steven with some random guy. And I knew it was my fault. I'd driven him to it. He'd never have done it if he hadn't found drugs in my pocket, and there were no good reasons or excuses for the drugs being there. So when Dinah called and asked me to brunch, I figured why not. If I wasn't going to sleep, I might as well get morning-drunk.

Dinah was my girl. Every fag needs a hag, and she was mine. When Aaron and I split and I set off to my new life in the big city, she'd even come along. For the first six months, we'd been inseparable, and she was my only social outlet at all. Movie nights and dinners and cocktails at my place were just enough socializing to keep me from going totally insane.

Then Dinah had gotten a boyfriend. Yes, even hags need love, as strange as it may sound. And although that meant less frequent outings with her gay bestie, Dinah made a point of holding to one of our traditions: Sunday brunch. When Steven and I started dating and he introduced me to the Duchess, Dinah and I gladly relocated our Sunday, and so that's where I found myself, emotionally hung over and Steven-less.

"So what did you do?" She'd never been one to hold back.

"It was ridiculous," I said, shaking my head. "I don't know what I was thinking. Wednesday night, I stopped in at the Palace for a drink after work and saw the Caterpillar, and figured, why not?"

"You gays and your drugs! On a Wednesday, Alex? Really?"

"It was dumb, I know. So anyway, Thursday, I was over at Steven's, and we'd just finished fucking—"

"I don't need the details there."

"Are you sure? I don't mind. I know you and Twitten probably need pointers."

"His name is Christopher, and our sex life is fine. More than I can say for yours right now."

"Oh, my sex life is fine, that's a different story."

"Alex, you didn't!"

"Guilty." I had the decency to look shamefaced at least. "Which story do you want first?"

She paused. "Who was the sex with?"

"The twins."

She choked on her mimosa. "You're kidding me."

"No."

"How did you get from wanting to propose to a threeway with Wonderland's wonder twins?"

"Steven found the stupid coke Baggie in my stupid pants after we fucked. He flipped."

"Understandably. You're an idiot."

"Thanks. You're a sweetheart."

"Anytime."

"He dumped me, Dinah. He said he wouldn't go through it again." Before me, Steven had dated a total druggie loser named Pierre. This wasn't the same; it wasn't a problem for me, or an addiction. Just a once-in-a-while itch that needed to be scratched. It was the first time since we had started dating that I had scratched it. Well, second maybe.

"Oh Alex, I'm sorry." Her hand was cold from her mimosa.

"What am I going to do, Dinah?"

"Have you called?"

"I tried. Voice mail."

"Has he called?"

"It was full, couldn't leave a message." I took a deep breath. "It gets worse."

"How can it?"

"I walked by on my way home from the club last night, and he was with someone."

"He was what?"

"I saw them through the curtains."

"He didn't!"

"He did."

"Well, even Steven, right?"

"That's what I thought. It doesn't make it feel any better."

"Well, you need to go talk to him, that's all."

"After brunch."

"Promise?"

"Yes."

"Okay good." She speared some sausage with her fork and looked at me with a mischievous grin. "Now, tell me about this threeway."

We had just finished brunch and ordered one last round of drinks when the door from the lobby opened and in came the twins, with Brandon and Allan. Brandon and Allan were still up from last night, as evidenced by their clothes and the glow paint still on their faces. The twins looked fresh as always; nothing tired them out. I knew that from having tried to tire them out just two nights before.

"Well look what we have here," Dinah said with a smirk.

"You hush your face."

"Yoohoo, booooooys!" she called out, waving them over. I kicked her under the table, and she laughed even as she yelped.

"Alex! Dinah!"

"Hey boys, what's up?"

"You bailed early last night," Jesse said, as they pulled up chairs and joined us. "Are you guys just getting here?" Colton asked.

"Just finishing actually," I said. "We were about to leave."

"Well, you have to stay now, we have gos-sip." Brandon delivered the last word with his normal sing-song flair.

"I'm not really in the mood for some faggy drama," I said, and got up.

"Sit down, Alex," Jesse said. "It's about Steven."

A thousand scenarios ran through my head. He was dead! He'd been coming to apologize for overreacting and he got hit by a bus and he was dead! Or the random trick he'd picked up off Grindr had turned out to be a homicidal maniac and chopped him up and they'd found pieces of him all over the gayborhood!

The most likely one—that they knew he had a trick and couldn't wait to tell me—of course occurred to me as well.

"What is it?" I asked.

"He's missing."

Chapter 8

The fuck? I sat there, dumbfounded. Here I thought we were going along in just a normal week of angst and drama in the gayborhood, and now what was this?

"What's this?" I asked. "What do you mean, missing?"

"We stopped by to get him on the way here. We hadn't seen him all weekend, and we figured, just because you two are fighting, doesn't mean he gets to ditch us all."

Colton carried on where Jesse left off. "But when we got to his house, his car was outside and the door was open. We went in, looked around, nothing. No sign of him."

"Did you call?"

"His phone was on his coffee table."

"What the . . ."

"When was the last time you saw him?"

"Last night." But was it? I saw two people there, but was one of them him? One must have been. You didn't kidnap a guy and then make out in his living room. Did you? "He was with someone." I told them what had happened. Dinah shook her head even more judgmentally this time around. I needed a new hag.

"Maybe he just went for a run and left his door open," Dinah said. "Or maybe his date did."

"Steven would never do that," I said. "He was anal about that.

Adorably anal." Brandon snickered at my unintended double-entendre. "Oh grow up," I snapped. Where could Steven be?

I took out my phone. "We told you he doesn't have his cell with him," Brandon said. I shushed him and dialed Steven's number. It rang. Oh wait, it was ringing right there at the table? Jesse took a cell out of his pocket.

"We brought Steven's with us," he explained. "In case he called it looking for it."

"You don't leave a brand new iPhone on a table with your door unlocked and wide open. Not with so many gay boys in the area looking for a cheap upgrade."

"Well you'd know about cheap upgrades, wouldn't you, Brandon?" I sneered at Allan.

"Hey now!"

Everyone started talking at once, and I couldn't be bothered to sort through the voices. I got up, took Steven's phone off the table.

"Where are you going?" Dinah asked.

"Steven's place to wait for him to get home. I'll talk to you guys later."

"Want me to go with you?" she asked.

"No, you stay here and visit. You can get brunch though." I stuck out my tongue. Yes, I was worried, but that wouldn't stop me from scoring a free meal. I was nervous, not stupid.

The boys had locked Steven's door when they left but I had a key. I knocked, waited, rang the bell, waited, and then let myself in. It was quiet, maybe too quiet, and as soon as I thought that, I realized I was just spooking myself. It was normal Sunday-morning quiet. I turned on his TV for background noise, not even caring that it was some church show. As the TV pastor pleaded for dollars, I looked around.

His keys were in the bowl by the door like always when he was home, but there was no sign of him. There was no sign of a struggle in the living room, nothing in the kitchen either. I walked into his bedroom. His sheets were rumpled, so he'd slept there at least. Well . . . maybe not slept, but he'd used the bed anyway. I went to the small garbage can by his nightstand—no condoms. That was good at least. Maybe he hadn't cheated.

Or had cheated but hadn't played safe.

No, that didn't sound like Steven. Any more than vanishing did, I added to myself. I lay down on the bed where I'd spent so many nights and let out a dramatic breath. I looked at his phone. It was locked, and I didn't know his code. I tried calling it, just to hear it ring, just to hear his voice on his voice mail.

"You've reached Steven. Leave me a message."

He'd clearly checked it since Saturday morning then. Where could he be? There was nothing really to do except wait for him to get home. I closed my eyes and breathed in his smell.

Chapter 9

"What are you doing here, Alex?" It was Steven's voice.

Oh good, *I thought,* a dream sequence, *and woke up. Well, the wake-up you do when you're sleeping inside a dream.*

Steven was sitting there on the bench, and looking over his shoulder at me. The sun was going down behind him, and the river was pink and gold. I'd been here before, many times. It was "our spot."

"I was looking for you," I said. "Where did you go?"

"I needed to get away for a while, that's all. This is where I go to think."

"Are you mad at me?"

"Very! I can't believe you had a threeway with Jesse and Colton and didn't invite me."

"What? I thought you were mad about the drugs."

"That too."

"Wait, who told you about the twins?"

"You did."

"When?"

"In this letter." He handed me a piece of paper. It was my writing sure enough, and a long drawn-out and detailed confession of my little Friday sexcapade.

"I didn't write this though." I handed it back to him.

"Oh." He ripped it up and threw the pieces into the air. They fell,

snowflakes around his head. "Want to go skating?" He held out his hand.

"I can't skate well, you know that."

"I won't let you fall." He grabbed my hand and led me out onto the pond. I wobbled, and he braced me. Soon enough, with my arms out to keep my balance (and break my fall), I was circling the pond next to him.

"I'm sorry, you know."

"For what?"

"For the drugs and the sex."

"We're gay. Isn't that what we do?"

"Not all of us."

"What else is there?"

I pulled the ring from my pocket. "This," I said.

"That's sweet, but you're not ready yet, clearly."

"I am. Trust me."

"I can't trust you, remember? Drugs? Sex?"

"Oh yeah."

"I've always known you were crazy, ever since you stalked me home that first day."

"It was supposed to be cute."

"It was," he said and smiled, "but still crazy."

"Where do we go from here?"

"Anywhere," he said, wrapping his arms around me from behind. He nudged my face with his chin. "Come on, take a step forward."

"We're too high." I could see below us, down the cliff, where the surf beat the rocks.

"I thought you liked being high."

"Hey!"

"Well . . ."

"Look, I'm scared," I said.

"Just one step. You can do it."

"Yeah, Alex, do it," came a woman's voice from behind us.

"Dinah? What are you doing here?"

"Came to check on you. I've known you longer than anyone else here. You need me."

"No I don't. We have our own lives now."

"She's right, Alex, you do need her."

"Maybe," I said with a shrug, and took a step forward, off the cliff. Steven held my hand as we floated through the night sky. "It got late."

"It's not that late. What time is it?"

I woke up, and checked the clock. It was four. I'd napped most of the afternoon. I wiped the drool off my face, glad that Steven wasn't here to see that, and checked my phone. Dinah had texted, wondering if I'd found Steven. I sent one back, saying no.

I grabbed some paper off Steven's desk and left him a note, asking him to please call me and let me know he was all right. I couldn't just hang out here all day without him. I knew I'd go crazy. I stuck the note on his fridge with a magnet, right next to a picture of us at the beach. I smiled as I looked at how happy we were.

Steven needed to hurry up and get his cute ass back home so we could be that happy again.

Chapter 10

When I got back to my place, I plugged my phone in so it wouldn't die and I wouldn't miss Steven's call, then fed my cat. I'd gotten him from Dinah years before, before I'd started dating Aaron, after a breakup with a pseudo-boyfriend named Chad. I don't think she understood that gay guys could, and often did, break up without hard feelings. We couldn't stay mad at each other; there weren't enough of us to go around. Straight people could break up and then completely lose track of their exes; gay people didn't have that luxury. There were only so many places gay men went, and even if you never bumped into your ex, you bumped into someone who knew him, someone who was only too happy to let you know how fabulous he was doing in your absence.

I had wanted a clean start, away from Aaron, from all our mutual friends, from all our mutual life. Dinah was the only piece that came with me, and she'd always been "mine" not "ours." She and Aaron got along great, sure, but her loyalty was to me.

I flopped down on my couch and turned on the TV. Griffin rubbed up against me, and I scratched his chin till he purred contentedly. I wished Steven would hurry the hell up and call. He had to be fine. Clearly, our fight, and maybe his date, had distracted him and he'd just left the door open. People didn't just vanish.

My phone rang, and I jumped up to get it, sending Griffin hissing to the floor. "Fuck!" I swore, seeing Jesse on the caller ID.

"No, I haven't heard from him," I said as I answered. "Have you?"

"No. What are you doing tonight?"

"Staying in and waiting for him to call."

"You need to come out. Keep distracted."

"I'm not in the mood for the club."

"We don't have to go dancing. Come watch a movie with Colton and I."

"Colton and me," I corrected without thinking, just like Steven always did to me. "And thanks but no thanks, I really just feel like staying in."

"Want us to come over? We could bring Chinese."

I hadn't had much for brunch, and hadn't eaten since, but I just didn't feel hungry, and I told Jesse that. He insisted though, and I eventually gave in, and within the hour, my buzzer rang.

"Come on up," I yelled into it, pressing the button on my intercom. "Well, Griffin, we have company." The buzzer rang again. "Didn't catch it?" I asked.

"Maybe you shouldn't be buzzing strangers into your building."

"Who is this? Colton?"

"There's a lot of crazies in the city. You need to be more careful."

"Who the fuck are you?" There wasn't any answer.

The fuck? I thought, as the buzzer rang again. "Look, who is this?"

"Is Chinese food for you! You angry when you hungry!" It was Jesse in his sad attempt at an accent.

"Do you guys see anyone around down there?"

"There was a guy leaving when our cab pulled up. Why?"

"Come on up," I said, buzzing them in. Crazies in the city indeed.

There was a knock on my door, and I looked through the peephole. Jesse and Colton were leaning against the opposite wall, rubbing each other suggestively. I opened the door, laughing. "Get in, you idiots, before the Walrus sees you and makes a complaint." The Walrus was my old fat homophobic neighbor with the most ridiculous moustache I'd ever seen.

They grabbed the brown bags of Chinese food off the floor and came in, kissing me on the cheek as they entered. "He still giving you a hard time?" Colton asked as I locked the door behind them.

"He's an idiot," I said. "Sometimes Steven and I make out in front of his door just so he has something to complain about."

"He hasn't called?"

"Not yet. Hey, who was leaving when you pulled up?"

"Just some guy. Why?"

I told them about the strange intercom conversation. When I was done, Jesse said, "He was just a guy. I didn't really pay attention."

"He had a nice ass though," Colton offered.

Jesse swatted him. "You would notice."

"Of course I noticed. But I wouldn't worry."

"I'm not."

"I was talking to Alex."

"I'm not either." I said, "It's just weird, with Steven missing."

"That's Brandon being dramatic. He's not *missing* missing, I'm sure."

"With his door wide open? That's strange."

"It's strange, definitely, but I wouldn't worry. Not yet."

"I'm trying not to."

"Good, let's eat," Jesse said, handing me one of the bags. "Egg roll?"

Chapter 11

Jesse and Colton got snuggly during the movie after we ate, and it drove home how much I was missing Steven. We hadn't ever gone this long without seeing each other, much less talking. I twiddled my phone in my hand, and I looked at it as much as I looked at the movie we were watching, but the old adage is true: "A watched iPhone never vibrates."

By the end of the movie, Jesse had fallen asleep with his head in Colton's lap. It was absolutely precious, and Colton smiled at me smiling at them. "Hey sweetie," he whispered, brushing Jesse's hair. "Wake up."

Jesse moaned and woke up with a pouty expression. "I was having a great dream, that my head was in your . . . oh it is." They kissed.

It was cute, corny, sweet, and made me miss Steven like crazy. "Get out, bitches. I need to sleep."

I walked them to the door. "Thanks for the Chinese," I said, as they grabbed their jackets, put on their shoes.

"He'll show up," Jesse said.

"He's probably calling you right now," Colton said, "and he'll apologize to your ass all night long."

"Or do something else to your ass all night long."

We laughed, and the door across the hall opened. My neighbor stood there, all receded hair, and shoulder hair, and moustache and man-boob.

"Oooh! We've awoken the Walrus!" Jesse half-whispered, and we all laughed as the Walrus glared.

"Do you ladies mind? It's late."

"It's eight-thirty, hunny," Colton minced.

The Walrus glared and slammed his door. "Can you not shut your door so hard, we're, like, trying to talk here!" Jesse, talking valley-girl, reduced us to tears.

"Okay guys, seriously."

"Text us in the morning?"

"Or anytime, if he calls?"

"Absolutely." We hugged and then they made out violently against the Walrus's door. Colton lifted Jesse up, faux-banging him against the wall, all grunts and moans and laughter. Then they walked down the hall laughing, their hands in each other's back pockets.

They'd always flirted with me and Steven, and they'd always been very open about their threesomes, and I'd always been curious. Steven wasn't into the idea, though, not that we'd ever really talked about it, but I could tell. For it to have happened so soon after our fight really did make me feel bad, but it was the gin and the coke and the sadness.

And the horniness, I admitted freely. Sex wasn't love, though; it could be meaningless, and frequently was. If Steven and I got back together—no, *when* Steven and I got back together—it wouldn't even be a blip on his radar. The drugs were more a betrayal than the sex. I mean, sure, we weren't like every other gay couple these days, doing the open thing, but . . . well, it was just sex.

Or was I just trying to convince myself of that? I'd never understood the gay guys who could do the open relationship thing, so why was I suddenly all about outside sex? Steven and I had agreed from the beginning we were monogamous (and really, with a hot catch like Steven, I didn't even want anyone else), but he had said we were done, and sex filled the void. In every way.

I checked my phone, and there was nothing. I hopped in the shower, and after, I checked my phone, and there was nothing. I lay there in bed, staring at my phone on my nightstand. I wondered if or when I should call the police. If he didn't get in touch by the time I was done with work on Monday, it would be time to panic.

The ring box sat on my dresser. It was the most recent crazy idea in the long line of crazy ideas that was my and Steven's relationship.

Everything had been going so amazingly well, and it just felt right. I was almost thirty, my wild oats were sowed and I was ready for it. But thirty and about to be engaged? I felt it sitting on my chest, and when a couple drinks after work didn't shake it loose, and the Caterpillar was there, I figured, why not? It wouldn't hurt anything. It didn't mean anything.

I nearly had myself convinced of that when I fell asleep.

I woke up to Griffin licking my face. "Scoot!" I snapped, tossing him gently onto the end of the bed. My room was cold and I could hear a rattling. The fuck? I wrapped myself up in my quilt and turned on the living room lights. My window blinds were blowing against each other.

"That's curious," I said out loud. I didn't remember leaving the window open.

Griffin sauntered out of the bedroom and meowed at me. "Did you open the window?" I asked him. He looked at me and meowed again. I closed the window, and looked out through the blinds. The city was alive below me, the lights, the late-night traffic. Somewhere out in that city, under those stars, Steven was probably laughing that I was worried.

I crawled back into bed, and Griffin hopped up onto the pillow next to me. I scratched the back of his head and yawned. "You better be okay," I said, and started to doze off. My iPhone's vibrating jerked me out of sleep. I grabbed it. Unknown number?

"Hello?" I answered.

"Is this Alex?"

"Yes, who is this?"

"Did you shut your window?"

"Who is this?"

"You don't want to catch a draft now, do you?"

"Look, if you don't tell me who this is, I'm hanging up and calling the cops."

"No, you look! Call the cops and Steven might not make it back to you."

"Alex!"

It was Steven's voice, calling from the background. I was suddenly wide awake. "Who is this? Let me talk to Steven."

"Steven is fine. How long he stays that way depends on you doing exactly what I tell you."

"What do you want?"

"I will call you in the morning. I'm watching you."

"I want to talk to Steven."

"Alex, I love you!"

"Sweet dreams, Alex." And the phone went dead.

I sat there, staring at the phone. Griffin meowed and rubbed against me. The voice had been unrecognizable, changing from one clearly faked accent to another. Someone, with bad accents and B-movie dialogue, had Steven. The fuck!

Chapter 12

I think I'd just fallen asleep when my alarm went off. My dreams, always strange, had been even stranger than normal. I was chasing Steven through a garden of giant flowers, and being chased in turn by my cat. No matter how loudly I called him, he kept running, and the flowers kept getting bigger and bigger. Just when I was about to grab hold of him, the flowers started changing into people I knew, and I lost Steven in the crowd.

Too many egg rolls.

There was nothing on my phone, and my window was still shut. I stuck my head out in the hallway, but saw nothing. Maybe I was paranoid, but it seemed warranted. I called in to work, took the day off. I almost called the police, but the voice had said not to.

Listening to voices so early in the day . . . it had to be a Monday. I put on some coffee, I made myself some toast, and I waited.

And watched some talk shows. And waited.

And watched some soap operas. And waited.

And paced. And ignored calls from Jesse and Colton. And paced some more. And waited some more. Why wasn't this guy calling me back? Was it all some game?

When the nightly news came on, I grabbed my coat and phone and went for a walk. There was no change at Steven's; his car was still there, and when I went in, it didn't look like anyone had been inside. His phone had died though, so I plugged it in for him. Of such little kindnesses is true love made: charging phones, and rescuing from crazed kidnappers.

Now that would be a grand gesture. He couldn't stay mad when I managed to rescue him. He'd be so happy to see me, his white knight coming to the rescue, everything would be forgiven, and we'd get that happy-ever-after.

I was just debating locking up when my phone rang. "Hello?"

"Any word?" It was Dinah.

"No."

"Are you going to the police?"

"Not yet. Maybe tomorrow." If I couldn't tell the police, maybe I shouldn't tell friends either.

"Where are you? Want me to come over?"

"I'm at Steven's. I was thinking of spending the night here."

"Awwww, that's cute. Call if you need to?"

"Will do." I'd no sooner hung up when it rang again. "Hi Jesse," I answered.

"Any news from your man?"

"Nothing."

"Colton and I think it's time to call the cops."

"I don't."

"But Alex . . ."

"Look guys, I can't. Trust me."

"Where are you right now?"

"At Steven's. I'm probably going to sleep over. In case he comes home."

"Did you go to work today?"

"No, he said he'd call . . ." I caught myself, but too late.

"Who? Steven?"

"Forget I said anything."

"What's going on, Alex?"

"Nothing, look, I gotta go."

I hung up. I was more nervous than I was letting on. The voice on the intercom, the window, the phone call . . . someone was watching me, and who knew how? Could they bug a phone? That was crazy, but not as crazy as kidnapping my soon-to-be fiancé.

Was it for money? I didn't have any to speak of. My job was decent, but not ransom-good. Why hadn't he called back yet? He'd said he'd call. Why hadn't he called? Was Steven okay?

The phone rang. It was Colton. Okay, their concern was sweet but they needed to let it go. My hands were shaking as I let it go to voice mail.

"This is ridiculous, Alex," I said aloud. "Call the police." I looked at my phone and took a deep breath, and just as I pressed nine, it rang, and I dropped it. "Shit!" I went to pick it up, and kicked it with my foot. It slid under the couch. I bent down to grab it, and pulled out a wallet. Tossing the wallet on the coffee table, I reached again for my phone, but by the time I found it, the ringing had stopped.

"Shit!" What if that was him? The missed call was unknown! What if I'd missed him? What if he hurt Steven?

The doorbell rang at the same time as my voice mail tone chimed. I called in as I walked to the door.

"You're not taking my calls. That seems stupid," the message began. I peered through the window. It was a police officer. *"Do not go to the cops. Do not call them. Do not answer the door."* My hand, reaching for the doorknob, paused. *"I will call back when they leave."* This guy was watching me right now!

I froze against the wall. The doorbell rang again, followed by a knocking. I barely dared to breathe. I waited. After a minute of silence, I moved slowly so I could see through the window. The officer was walking down to his car. I waited to move again until he got in and drove away. The car had no sooner turned off Steven's street than the phone rang.

"I didn't do it!" I answered. "I didn't call them."

"Lucky for you I believe you. This is the situation, Alex. I have something you want, you have something I want."

"What? Anything!"

"Check the mailbox."

I opened the door and reached into the mailbox. It was a flyer for Wonderland. "What is this?" I asked. "Some drag show? You kidnapped Steven to get me to go to a drag show?"

"Flip the paper, pretty boy."

On the back it read "White Night Tuesday 10 P.M."

"What does that mean?"

But my phone was silent. What was going on now?

Chapter 13

I had no idea what White Night was. A place? A party? I googled it, but nothing came up. At least, nothing that made sense. If Google didn't know, then where could I turn? There was only one answer.

I texted Jesse: **do you know what white night is?** and then I waited for his reply. Jesse knew loads of useless trivia, and if white nights had anything to do with anything or anywhere local, he'd know about it.

His reply came: **why do you wanna know about that?**

You know what it is?

Well it's a bathhouse thing . . . since when are you a tubs queen?

Bathhouse? Really?

You can just come over to our place if you're horny waiting for Steven to get home.

What is it?

Just a circuit party they have at the baths once in a while.

How often?

Actually, I think it's tomorrow night. Why are you asking?

Someone mentioned it, I didn't know what it was.

Well we haven't been in years so if you go, let us know!

I'm not going to the bathhouse.

Sure you're not :P

I stopped replying. A bathhouse circuit party? What kind of kidnapper sends you to a bathhouse? I'd never been, but from what I understood, it was just a sex club. With that in mind, I re-googled "White Night" and there, on the second page (yes, there is a second page to Google results), was "White Night: gay dance party at the bathhouse." They were bringing in the Hatter so at least the music would be good, but what did it mean? Was I just supposed to go?

And I still felt like I should call the cops.

My phone buzzed. It was Colton, asking if I was going to the baths without them. I replied negatively. Apparently, I would be going, but I definitely didn't need the twins tagging along. They were a distraction in the best of times. I couldn't imagine getting anything accomplished if they were wandering around in thin white towels.

Whatever the case, it was a day away. And I just hoped it was the right thing. It seemed innocent and easy enough, curious and strange, yes (and was it strange that I was a bit curious?), but innocent and easy, and if all I had to do was go to a circuit party at a bathhouse to get Steven back, well, I was more than willing to endure what I had to endure.

I went into work the next day, but my mind wasn't really on it, understandably. I watched the hours on the clock tick away, until it was time for lunch. I met Dinah at a greasy spoon around the corner, and ordered the unhealthiest meal I could find on the menu. I was starving, and had to keep my strength up.

"I can't believe you haven't gone to the police yet," Dinah said, helping herself to some of my poutine.

"Trust me, I can't."

"What aren't you telling me, Alex?"

I glanced around. The place was a madhouse at lunch, it was rattling dishes and people talking and bad eighties pop being piped in through the stereo. I had to tell someone, and Dinah was my hag after all. I told her everything, about the man at my intercom, and the phone calls, and the flyer in the mailbox.

"Someone is fucking with you," she said when I was done. "It's got to be some sort of big gay joke, because it just can't be real. Everything is so over the top with you people."

I grinned. "That's what I'm hoping too, but what if—"

"Alex. You are being sent to a bathhouse for a circuit party. It's not like you've been sent Steven's finger in the mail. It's a joke, a bad joke sure, but a joke. Go along with it, and whoever it is, tell him, when you find out, that he needs to stop watching such bad TV and get some better ideas."

"So you think Steven is in on it?"

"It just seems too ludicrous to take seriously. Are you legitimately worried?"

"Well I was, but actually saying it all out loud, it does seem pretty preposterous, doesn't it? Maybe I shouldn't even go, stop playing along. Steven and whoever will get bored, and then the joke's on them."

"Oh no, don't do that, you have to go."

"You just want to know what a bathhouse is all about."

"Well yeah, it's not fair you gays get a place all set up for casual sex like that."

"Bored with Twitten?"

"His name is Christopher, and no, he's amazing in bed." She stole some more fries. "But I wouldn't say no to a threeway. Why should you get to have all the fun?"

"Sorry honey," I laughed, "but I don't think your dick is big enough for Jesse."

I felt a lot better after that, and managed to actually make some headway into the pile of loan applications, et cetera, piling up on my desk at the bank. That had to be it. It was some joke or test or something, maybe even Steven's twisted way of punishing me for my drug fuckup the week before. I finished work, hit the gym for an hour to work off the bloating, disgustingly delicious lunch I'd inhaled, hit the tanning bed, then went home to feed Griffin and wait for ten.

Jesse called around seven. "So are you going tonight?"

"I told you I'm not."

"Who mentioned it?"

"I don't remember. It's really not important."

"We won't judge you, Alex. I mean, we're the last people to judge anyone else's relationship. Open is the new married. The couple that plays together, stays together. Just be safe, okay?"

"I'm not going to the bathhouse, Jesse!"

He laughed. "Have you heard from Steven?"

"No, but I'm not worried. The more I think about it, the more I'm sure he is just taking some time to cool off."

"If you say so. I gotta go, Colton just got home, and I'm horny."

"Thanks for sharing."

"Have fun at White Night." He hung up, laughing, and I started to get ready to have fun at White Night.

Chapter 14

There was an alley behind Wonderland. On a weekend night, you'd normally find people smoking joints and sucking dick in the shadows. On a Tuesday, it was pretty empty. Wonderland itself had been quiet as I walked by, and too bad. I could've used a stiff drink.

At least it was about to be over.

Like I said, I'd never been to a bathhouse but did have some idea how they worked and what to expect. When I got to the check-in window, I bought myself a room, and the guy behind the counter handed me a towel, a condom, and little packet of lube. I wouldn't be needing any of them. I was just here to figure out what was going on. I got buzzed into the dark halls, and was immediately hit by the humidity.

I assumed he would call me again, so I kept my phone on me. There were people of all ages and shapes wandering the halls in their towels. They gave me appraising looks, but did any of them look at me unusually long? Was one of these guys the reason I was here?

I found my room and sat down on the bed, making sure the door was locked behind me. It was only nine-thirty, I had some time to kill. According to their website, the Hatter started spinning at ten. Right now, the music was canned satellite house, generic, flat, barely loud enough to conceal the grunts that floated from other rooms.

I couldn't help being a bit turned on. Even if none of the guys I'd seen so far had been hot, moans from the darkness could be made by anyone.

Eventually, curiosity got the best of me, and I changed into my towel so I could wander the halls. I didn't want to be conspicuous after all. I wasn't the ripped leanness of Brandon or the sculpted beauty of Jesse and Colton but I was trim and fit compared to most of the other guys that were there. I tucked my phone into my towel and pulled the towel tight so it wouldn't fall off.

It was exactly what I'd expected, dark and steamy and a bit grungy, and a bit sexy. There was some hot porn showing on random TVs, and shapes in the darkness touching, melding, joining. Down one hall, I could see the metal and leather of a sling hanging from the ceiling in an alcove. I went the other way, my hand on my phone. Why wasn't this guy calling? It had to be nearly ten.

I rounded a corner and bumped into a guy. "Sorry," I said, but he groped my dick through my towel. I pushed him away, and spun around, coming face to face with Allan.

"Hey!" I said, feeling immediately awkward at running into someone I knew. "Is Brandon with—"

BAM! He had me pinned against the wall. "It's Alex, right?"

"Whoa dude, what the . . ."

"You didn't see me here, got it? It has nothing to do with you."

I shoved the twink off me, surprised he'd managed to pin me at all. His eyes were a bit wild, come to think of it, and I suspected it wasn't just ketamine that the boy liked to take.

"You're crazy!"

He grabbed my arm. "I'm fuckin' serious. You tell Brandon you saw me here, and I will cut you."

The fuck? I had enough going on, I did not need to deal with the threats of some sketchy kid. I walked away, not daring to look back until I'd reached the end of the hall. When I did glance back, Allan was still glaring at me. I rounded the corner and took out my phone, texting Brandon that I had to tell him something.

I went back to my room, my curiosity more than sated for now. It was just after ten. Whatever was going to happen, was going to happen soon. If this was all a joke, I was officially no longer amused. And if it wasn't, I was going straight to the cops. Enough was enough.

My phone rang. "Hello?"

"You came. That's good."

"Look, I'm tired of this, is this all just some joke?"

"It's no joke, Alex. I don't think you and Steven are a good match. I don't think you think that you and Steven are a good match."

"You're nuts. I love Steven!"

"Do you? Do you really?"

"I'm calling the police, this is crazy."

"Don't hang up the phone, Alex!" In the background, I heard Steven scream. His voice cut into me, full of pain and terror. I was convinced: This wasn't a joke. "You hang up the phone, you go to the police, you do anything other than what I tell you, and the next time you see Steven, it will be at his funeral."

"Alex, I love you!" Steven's voice, pleading at me, cut even deeper than his scream.

"Let me talk to him! What are you doing to him? What do you want?" Tears stung at my eyes.

"I want you to have a good time. Go downstairs, dance, do drugs, get fucked. Do whatever you want."

"I'm not really in the mood, I just want Steven back."

"Steven wants you to have a good time. Don't you, Steven?"

"Yes! Alex! Just do it!"

Was it some kind of test? Was he still playing with me? "No."

Steven screamed through the phone.

"Stop it! What are you doing to him?"

"Your boyfriend cut himself shaving, Alex. He don't bleed so pretty."

"What do you want from us?"

"I want you to prove for me what I've always known. You don't love."

"I do! I love him!"

"Did you love him when you were having your threesome the other night? Did you love him when you were doing drugs like some loser?"

"Yes! Even then!"

"You don't know what love is, Alex! Go dance and have sex. That's all you're really good for."

"I will! I promise I will! Just let him go."

"And don't think you can just say you're going to. I'll know."

How could he know? Cameras? I scanned around my room. I couldn't see anything. "Let him go, I'll dance, I promise."

"I will call you in two hours." The phone went dead. I started to dial 911, but paused. What if he could see? What if he did know? This wasn't a joke and he wasn't playing around. What the hell was I supposed to do?

Chapter 15

Leaving my phone on the bed, I wandered back out into the hall. It was louder now, and busier, and instead of just trolls in towels, there was a bigger mix of people, posses of twinks and muscle boys in designer undies talking and laughing as they walked about, dancing in corners to the Hatter's sick beats. Mirrorballs had exploded into action, and fog was being pumped in from somewhere. In minutes, the hallways of the baths had become a dance club.

I wasn't in the mood to dance or cruise. What kind of psychopath had Steven? Was he watching me even now? I couldn't see cameras in the hall. The faces all around me were happy, some made eye contact. Did they know something? Was one of them watching my every move? I thought about the choices I had.

If he knew what I was doing, and he did seem to know, then how could I not do what he'd said? Dance, hook up? No, how could I even think about having a good time, much less getting a hard-on, when Steven was being held, even tortured, by some loony? All I wanted was to know he was okay. All I wanted was to have him here with me. The only way for that to happen was to hook up at a bathhouse? How was this my life? It was surreal. It was wrong. I couldn't do it. I wouldn't do it.

What choice did I have? The man on the phone had made it crystal clear. This wasn't my choice. This wasn't cheating. This is what I had to do to rescue the man I loved. And the part of my brain that kept telling me to keep telling myself that, well, that part needed to shut up.

Suddenly, I felt like I was about to throw up and ran to the bathroom. I bent over the sink, spitting up, my stomach heaving. This was crazy! How was I supposed to have fun?

"You all right there, friend?"

I looked into the mirror and saw the Caterpillar behind me. Of course he'd be here. He followed the club kids, so even though he was straight, a big dance party at a gay bathhouse would have too many business opportunities for him to pass up. He was wearing his jacket, even in the heat. I let out a disgusted grunt. He was the last person I wanted to see . . . or was he? There was no way I could have fun sober . . . and maybe with a little help, I could forget.

"Need a party favor?"

No, it was stupid, I thought. What if the guy called back and I was too fucked up to respond? On the other hand, at least I wouldn't be freaking out with worry.

"What do you recommend?"

He pulled out a little pink pill. "Take this," he said, pushing it between my lips like communion. I washed it down with a handful of water.

It didn't take long to feel the heat radiating through me, from the steam, from the pill. I couldn't remember the last time I'd taken Ecstasy. I didn't know people even still did. Wonderland was all K and G and coke. The lights were brighter now, and I found my way downstairs, where the Hatter had set up a temporary DJ booth. He nodded at me as I passed through the doorway into a cloud of steam.

It was the wet area. Showers lined one wall. In some, guys rinsed off. In others, guys got off, stroking themselves, or getting head. They watched me as I walked by, and I watched them watching me. I was hard under the towel, and the steam filled my lungs. Lasers bounced off the tiles, green and red, and I followed their lines into the steam room.

It was dark here, and the music was muted. The steam was thick, and occasionally I'd pass someone in the fog. They would touch me, or I would touch them. They were faceless. I was faceless. My mouth was dry, and my dick was hard. I needed to sit down.

I found an alcove with a little bench, off the main path of the steam maze. I pulled off my towel and wiped the sweat from my face.

My hands brushed over my chest, goose bumps in the steam. I chuckled. I'd forgotten how good it could feel, Ecstasy. In the warm glow, the "why" of what I was doing was barely there. I was floating.

I felt someone else's hand on my leg. I couldn't see his face. His face didn't matter. My eyes were closed and it felt too good. His mouth was wet and cold in the heat. My hands were in his hair. I grunted. His mouth pulled off me. "Don't stop," I told him.

"Alex?"

I recognized that voice, through the Ecstasy fog. Who was it? I blinked, letting my eyes readjust to the poor light. I knew the face between my legs. "Aaron? What the . . ."

"I knew your dick was familiar," he laughed nervously.

"What are you doing here?"

"I'm up here for work. Figured I could have a little fun, too." He paused, sat down next to me. I could feel his knee against my thigh. "Why are you here?"

Why was I here? I couldn't focus. All I could think of was how good he'd felt. I pulled his mouth to mine. He let out a moan. Our tongues danced to the music, in the steam, in the dark. It was familiar and new and warm and wet, slick and fast and hard. I let myself fly.

Chapter 16

Later, in the shower, I couldn't believe what I'd done. Aaron smiled at me from the next showerhead, and I buried my face in the water so I wouldn't have to look at him. We hadn't seen each other in so long, and to run into each other there, of all places, that night, of all nights! I couldn't help but look at him though, the body I'd spent so many years next to. I could feel myself twitch again.

"Want to go get a drink?" he asked.

"Where?" I said.

"There's a bar just upstairs. They licensed it for the evening."

That, I hadn't known. Gin would have been a safer choice than E. "Sure," I said.

With towels wrapped around our waists, we walked upstairs, past the Hatter, who was absorbed in spinning. We didn't talk. Aaron put his hand on my shoulder as we went up, and I pulled away. What had I done? The pill was worn off, and my brain was crying out in panic again. What about Steven? This is what the guy on the phone had wanted me to do though. Did he know? Was it enough to get Steven released?

"Rum and Coke?" Aaron asked me, at the makeshift bar they'd set up.

"Gin," I said, "with cran if they have it."

"You've changed your drink."

"A lot's changed."

"You still give great head." He smiled at me.

"Thanks, but it was stupid."

"It doesn't mean anything. Part of the party." He ordered our drinks, passed me mine. "Want to go to my room?"

I had to check my phone, check the time, see if he'd called again. "No, let's go to mine."

Aaron grinned. "Okay."

"Look, it's not what you think."

"Relax, Alex, it was a blow job at the bathhouse. It doesn't mean anything."

"I'm with someone now."

"Oh? Is he here? I could be up for a threeway."

A threeway? That wasn't the Aaron I remembered. Not that it mattered right now. That wasn't what this was about. "No, it's not like that. We don't do that." How much did I want to tell Aaron? He was my ex after all. But we'd also shared so much, and maybe an outsider's opinion would be good. I unlocked my room and we sat down on the bed. I couldn't help but notice his dick flop out of his towel. It was as beautiful as I remembered it.

"So why are you here, if you have a boyfriend?"

"We're going through something."

"So you thought this would help?"

"No, that's not it."

"Well, it doesn't matter. It was a treat running into you. I've missed you." He put his hand on my leg. It felt good, and not from the E. Six years we'd been together.

"It's nice seeing you, too." We sipped our drinks. It was eleven-thirty, I saw on my phone, so he should be calling back soon.

"How long have you been together?"

"A while now. What about you?" I asked, desperate to change the subject. "Anyone special?"

"If there was, would I be here?" He paused. "Sorry, I'm not judging."

"Yes you are."

"Maybe a bit."

"It's complicated."

"It always is with you, Alex. You can't ever let things be simple."

"How do you know it's my fault?"

"I just assumed."

"Well don't."

"So it's him?

"Look, I don't want to talk about it."

"I'm okay with not talking too." He moved in to kiss me. I pushed him back.

"Aaron, I can't . . ."

"What's the big deal? We already fooled around." He took my hand, put it on his dick. He was hard again. "I want to fuck you." His voice was husky, like how he got when he was horny. I remembered all the times he'd used that voice on me. I'd never been able to say no to it. We were practically naked, in a bathhouse, and we'd already done so much, and it wasn't my fault, I hadn't wanted to be here.

He leaned in to kiss me again. I didn't push him off.

Chapter 17

Drugs and sex. They went together in my head, even after six clean(ish) months with Steven. Back in college, just coming out and ready to explore what being gay was all about, it was nothing to go out, get fucked up, get fucked, and do it all over again the next day. Booze, coke, E, it was all a blur, and the boys and their bodies and their bulges and their butts, that was a blur too.

When Aaron and I started dating, it was good-bye to that lifestyle, and at the time, I was happy to see it go. But as the relationship became boring and predictable, I looked back on those younger days with increasing fondness. The morning-after panicking over whether we'd played safe, the throb of the hangover as I tried to remember his face, the shame that would hit me out of the blue sometimes, all of that got glossed over, and I just remembered how fun it was.

When Aaron and I split, and I moved, I wasn't ready to plunge back into that world, but then came last Pride. Dinah and I went to the parade and got caught up in the rainbow celebration of it all, and for some reason, I decided to (re)download Grindr while we were at the beer gardens. *BING! BING! BING!* My phone went mad—nothing like being fresh meat in a sea of horny, hungry homos—and they were all just feet away! I messaged one back, a sexy Spanish-looking guy, and we made plans to meet up at his place. I ditched Dinah ASAP (friends over fucks, unless it's Pride, right?). When I got to the guy's place, he asked if I partied. It had been a while, but sure, why not?

And that's how I met the Caterpillar. He came over, in the same jacket he always wore, some cross between ringmaster and pimp daddy. After he left, Hunky Spaniard and I dumped out some blow and then got to blowing, making sure we were flying high but not high enough for coke dick. Before I left, for some reason, I asked for the Caterpillar's number.

I had called a few times after that. I wasn't in the mood for bars or parties or Grindr hookups, but sometimes, after a long week at work, it was nice to just kick back at home, with a gram of coke and the boys of Sean Cody. Sex and drugs.

After Aaron fucked me, we lay there, and he held me. "How long are you in town for?" I asked.

"Not sure yet, depends how quick I get my work done." He kissed my shoulder. "And maybe if there's a reason to stay longer."

I sat up. "It was nice, Aaron. Very nice. But it can't happen again. I'm with Steven now."

"Do you love him?"

"Yes. I know that seems stupid to say after what we just did, but I do."

He stood up, and wrapped his towel around his waist. "I'm happy for you then, Alex, I really am." He saw my phone, and picked it up. "Here's my number though," he continued, as he punched it in, "in case you just want to get coffee or something while I'm here."

"I'd like that."

He leaned in and kissed me, maybe longer than was appropriate. Or maybe not given he'd just been inside me. "Call me." And he left.

It was crazy, but it's not like we'd had a bad breakup. It just had gotten so boring. There'd been no surprises anymore. We knew everything. We didn't challenge each other, didn't inspire each other. I looked at his number in my phone, and my finger hovered over the DELETE CONTACT button. It couldn't hurt to keep though. Maybe being friends was the healthy thing to do. I'd have to ask Dinah.

I lay there, staring at my phone and trying to ignore the mess of emotions inside my head. Finally, the phone rang, unknown number. "Well done, Alex," he said, when I answered.

"I did what you wanted. Now let him go."

"You need to tell him."

"What?"

"He needs to hear it from you, and don't skimp on the details."

"That's sick." I heard the phone volume change, could tell he'd put me on a speakerphone.

"Alex!"

Steven's voice cut me like a knife. I could still feel Aaron inside me. Aaron. Steven. My head spun. "Steven, are you okay?"

"Tell him what you did, Alex. Tell him where you are."

"I'm at the bathhouse. I had sex. He told me I had to. He told me he'd hurt you."

"In detail, Alex."

"Why? You got what you wanted, isn't that enough?"

"Not even a little bit."

"It's okay, Alex, I forgive you." He was crying. I was too.

"Tell him!"

I did, without mentioning that it had been Aaron. That was unnecessary pain. I could hear Steven sobbing, but every time I tried to hold back something, the man kept at me: "Is that it? Was there more?" Until finally I said, "That's everything! What more do you want me to say? You know everything!"

"Do we? Tell Steven how much you liked it, how much you enjoyed that stranger fucking you like the trash you are."

Steven was sobbing, I was sobbing. "Fine! I liked it! Let him go!"

"Oh no, Alex, that's not how it works. It's not done yet."

"You promised . . ."

"I promised nothing! Besides, what do promises mean? You said you loved this waste of skin here, and what was that worth? You got on your knees and got fucked by the first guy that came along."

"What choice did I have?"

"There's always a choice, Alex! You could have let me kill him without him ever having to know what a disgusting faggot you are." His laugh was a cold, harsh bark. "I'll be in touch. Don't forget, no cops!"

The phone went dead, and I was crying. What did he want now? What would he ask of me? And would Steven ever forgive me? It was true, what he'd said. Maybe not tonight, but Friday with the twins? I was drunk and high and not thinking about Steven then at all. Well, hardly at all.

I needed to get home. I got dressed, ignoring the people all around me as I left. The air outside was cold after the heat of White Night. I rounded the corner onto the street. Wonderland was still quiet, but open. I needed a drink. I went downstairs and smiled when I saw Brandon behind the bar. A friendly face was exactly what I needed.

He saw me, leapt over the bar, and I didn't have time to duck as his fist collided with my face.

Chapter 18

"What the . . . !" My head was ringing!

"Just because you and Steven are having problems, you have to get all up in my relationship with Allan?" He smacked me again.

"Ow! Stop that!" I grabbed his wrists. "What are you talking about?"

"Allan told me you tried picking him up."

"What? I did no such thing!"

"Why would he make that up, Alex?"

"Look, he's psycho. I saw him at the baths tonight and—"

"The baths? What the hell, Alex? When did you turn into such a whore?"

"That's not the point. Allan was there, he was high and crazy."

"You're just covering your ass. Fuck, Alex, if you'd wanted him that bad, you could've taken me up on that offer Saturday."

"I don't want Allan! I have no interest in Allan whatsoever! I have a boyfriend!"

"Which doesn't stop you from having threeways and from cruising the tubs. Steven's a lucky guy! No wonder he left!"

"Fuck you, Brandon."

"You're a slut, Alex."

"You're really going to take the word of some sketchy twink you just met over me? Great friend there, Brandon."

"Go to hell, Alex. Get out."

"Fuck you, I'm here for a drink, so why don't you hop behind the bar and make me one."

"You're a loser."

"And a slut. I get it. Drink now, please."

Brandon glared at me, and stormed behind the bar. I sat down at my normal spot, vibrating. On top of everything else, I had some kid stirring up stupid gay drama? And Brandon was buying it? Fuck them both. "Where's that drink?"

"Right here, asshole. Drink this!" I turned, and SPLASH! I blinked away the cranberry juice.

I had gin at home. I did not need that shit. Flipping Brandon off, I stomped upstairs, wiping my face. I dug around in my jacket pocket for a Kleenex, but all I had was the show flyer. It was for the Queen of Hearts show coming up Friday night. Another stupid drag show at the stupid gay bar? No thanks. I tossed it into the gutter.

I was done with the scene! As soon as I got Steven back, that was it. We were moving to some small town where we were the only two gay people and where there was no drama. I let my mind wander as I walked home, picturing our house, even decorating. It would be wonderful. Maybe Dinah and Christopher would come out for Thanksgiving, but it would just be me and Steven.

All I had to do was get him back.

I let myself into my building and waited for the elevator. I was still shaking. I checked my phone—nothing—and I figured nothing was going to happen overnight. And even if it did, I needed downtime, needed a break from it all. The most that would happen would be Brandon getting high at work and sending me bitchy text messages anyway.

I got off at my floor and stopped short.

"What the . . ."

Spray-painted across my apartment door, in big green letters, was FAGGOT WHORE. I kicked the wall, slammed my hands against it. "Fuck fuck fuck fuck fuck fuck fuck fuck fuck fuck!" I swore, kicking the wall again with every fuck. Was it Allan? Was it this crazy guy bent on destroying my life?

The door across the hall opened. "Do you have any idea what time it is?"

"Not right now, Walrus. Fuck off!"

The Walrus took in my door. "I see I'm not the only one that knows the truth."

"What did you say?" I took a step toward him. "Did you see who did this? I know you fucking sit in there peering through your peephole, you sick fuck. Probably getting off on everyone else's life."

He sneered at me with such loathing. "Fag." And he shut the door.

"Fuck you!" I screamed, and proceeded to kick his door for a change, until my foot was sore.

It was too much. I let myself into the apartment. Griffin was meowing at the door. I slid down against the wall to join him, and as I scratched his back, I started to cry.

Chapter 19

I was thirteen. I was walking home from school when they went by on their bikes. "Fag!" they yelled as they pedaled past. I ignored them. I always ignored them. It was just a word, I told myself. Just a word, and it didn't mean anything. It wasn't even about me.

That day, they didn't just yell "fag" as they rode by. They circled back and did it again. And then again. I started to walk faster. I couldn't run. They'd be on me if I ran. I was only two blocks from home. They'd get bored. They were jerks. They'd get bored. Why weren't they getting bored?

They started to circle me. "Fag!" "Queer!" "Homo!"

"Stop it!" I yelled.

"Ah, look, the sissy is crying." They were getting off their bikes. I tried to run through them, but one tripped me.

"Leave me alone!" I was crying. I hated crying. I jumped to my feet. My hands were bleeding.

"Faggot faggot faggot faggot," they chanted, in a circle around me, pushing me back and forth.

Eventually they stopped, and I ran home. I hid in the backyard until I stopped crying. My dad hated it when I cried. And what could I say? That guys were picking on me? He called me sissy too, when he was angry. It was just words. I didn't need to cry.

* * *

I was fifteen. His name was Nathan. He was blond-haired and blue-eyed and slim and smooth and wonderful. We were in his room studying, when he asked me if I wanted to watch some porn. I was immediately hard. We were sitting there at his desk, and it was the first time I'd ever seen sex. I was watching the guy on the screen, and the guy beside me, and not the girl at all.

"Isn't she hot? Look at those tits!"

I just nodded.

Out of the corner of my eye, I could see him rubbing his crotch. I saw my fingers reaching out toward him. I couldn't help myself. I touched his thigh.

He jerked away. "Dude, what are you doing?"

I jumped to my feet. "I . . . I . . ."

"What are you, some kind of faggot?"

"No . . . I . . ."

"Get out of my room!"

I ran from his house, crying. "Faggot!" he called after me. It was just a word. Why did it still make me cry?

I was seventeen and his name was Taylor. He didn't pull away when I went to touch him. Quite the contrary. He touched me right back. Every weekend, in the quiet darkness of my room, we explored each other's bodies. He was my best friend and my first love.

I knew I was gay by then. I'd admitted it. Only Taylor and Dinah knew though. I wasn't ready to tell my parents, and neither was he. No one really called us that at school anymore. In accepting it was true, we'd stopped reacting with fear and tears, and the joke wasn't as fun for the bullies anymore.

Our teacher had asked me to help Taylor with his math homework, and things had just gone from there. The first time we kissed, we were both laughing so hard, it didn't really work out. But then he looked at me with his deep brown eyes, and I brushed his hair off his face (he had this bang that always flopped over his eye), and things got really quiet, and a lot less funny, and I think I fell in love the first time our lips met.

We had been together for all of eleventh grade, and the summer, and our senior year was starting, and we had made so many plans. We were going to come out after high school. We were going to go to college together. We would sit in his room, or in my room, or anywhere we could be alone, and we would dream. And kiss. And more. But mostly we would dream. Together.

One night, we were doing a lot more than dreaming when his bedroom door opened and the lights came on. We tried to pull a blanket over us, screaming at his mom to close the door. She stammered an apology and we could hear her run down the stairs. We scrambled to get dressed, swearing.

We heard his dad roar from downstairs. "A fucking faggot? No son of mine!"

"Quick! Out the window!" Taylor said, and I grabbed my jacket, and I kissed him on the lips as I slipped out the window. Climbing down the tree that led up to his bedroom, I could hear his dad slam into his room, yelling. I could hear his mom crying. I could hear Taylor crying. I wanted to go back up, to tell him it was just a word. I wanted to tell him not to cry.

I was twenty-two, and Dinah and I laughed as we walked down the street. We were done with college, and our lives were all ahead of us, and what better way to celebrate than drinking and dancing at the gay bar? It was a Friday night, and we were young, and we were beautiful.

"I told you we should have come earlier," Dinah said, as we rounded the corner and saw a lineup. "You always take so long getting pretty."

"But it will be worth it if I meet some great guy."

"What about that Aaron guy you went on a date with?"

"We'll see. It went well. I haven't called him yet."

"Why not?"

"I can't seem needy. He can call me."

"If you like him, just call him."

"FAGGOTS!" A bottle came flying out of a car as it sped by, smashing on the sidewalk. We jumped away, as did the other people in line.

"Assholes!" Dinah yelled after them.

"Don't bother, Dinah. It's just a word."

"It pisses me off though. What are we doing to them? We're just here."

"That's all it takes sometimes."

Chapter 20

I woke up, still at my door. It was the middle of the night, and my neck was sore, my head foggy. As I grabbed myself a glass of water, and put down some food for Griffin, I turned on my phone. It was just what I'd expected: a bunch of poorly spelled and bitchy texts from Brandon, and one from Jesse just checking in. I turned it off again.

I crawled into my bed and pulled the blankets up over my head. I never thought about Taylor. I never let myself think about Taylor. I'd run home from his house that day, and told my parents everything, and even though my mom cried and my dad was quiet, they both hugged me and told me I was still their son.

Taylor hadn't been so lucky.

The next morning at school, he wouldn't even look at me. Well, he couldn't even look at me, with his black and swollen eye. I tried to talk to him, and he pushed me away. I tried calling him that night, and his mom asked me not to call there again. I didn't know what to do, but I needed to see him, needed to know he was all right.

I snuck out of my room in the middle of the night and ran to his place, climbed the big tree outside and tossed a couple rocks lightly against his window. Eventually, he opened it up.

"You can't be here, Alex!" he whispered at me.

"I had to know you're okay."

"I'm fine. Go."

"I don't believe you. Can I come in?"

"No!" His expression was terrified. "We can't hang out anymore."

"I love you, Taylor."

"Don't say stuff like that. It's wrong."

"No, it's not! It's real. Two hearts, one heart, remember?"

"You need to go, Alex. It's over."

"Just tell me you're okay."

"I'm going to be fine," he said. His terror had faded, and his face was just empty now. "Bye, Alex."

"I love you," I said again, to the closing window.

I walked home, thinking about how good it felt to touch him, to kiss him, to be naked with him. That hadn't even been the best part, though. He'd made me feel not so alone. Just knowing that there was at least one other person in the world who felt the same way I did, it made a difference. We just needed to finish high school, and get on with the next part of our lives.

I tossed around in my bed. I couldn't get comfortable. Why was I thinking about that? It was so long ago. It didn't matter anymore. I flipped onto my side and buried my face in the pillow, but I could still see it.

Her name was Mrs. Whiting, and she was our homeroom teacher, and she came in that morning, and her face was gray, and I knew something bad had happened even before she said it. I didn't even hear the words, it was all slow motion. The girl in front of me started to cry. I needed to talk to Dinah. I got up, barely conscious that I was moving.

"Alex, take your seat, please," Mrs. Whiting called after me.

"He's sad about his boyfriend," Nathan said as I passed by him. My grief was replaced by rage, and I spun around. The next thing I knew, Nathan was underneath me and my fists were pummeling him. People grabbed my arms, dragged me off him. I melted into a pool of tears. I couldn't believe Taylor was gone.

I flipped onto my other side. I saw me and Dinah, all in black. We were all in black, the whole class, and Nathan's eyes were both black as he glared at me from the other side of the room. I didn't look at the coffin. I didn't look at the flowers. I didn't want to think about the boy in that coffin, the boy who had turned a gun on himself, the boy I loved. I stared at a spot on the floor, and I didn't cry. Dinah held my hand, and her head was on my shoulder and I could smell her shampoo.

* * *

My alarm clock went off. I turned my phone back on and called in to work. I was in no shape to go in, and it didn't seem like it was going to change. I took the rest of the week off. I had plenty of holidays coming up. Steven and I had been talking about New Year's on the Mayan Riviera. Now, that seemed unlikely.

I got up, hopped in the shower. The steam reminded me of White Night, made me think of Aaron. After Taylor, I never said "I love you" to another guy until Aaron. And there'd been quite a few guys. College had really been such a blur of bars and booze and boys and blow, weekdays busy in class, weekends busy in bed. I had gotten around. Maybe my apartment door was right. Maybe I was just a faggot whore.

I texted Dinah, and made plans to meet her for lunch. I texted the twins, and we made plans to meet up for wings that evening. And then I sat there, wondering what to do. I angrily flipped through channels. I cranked Lady Gaga and screamed along with "Speechless." I paced. Finally, I decided enough was enough, and I had to get out.

I made a point of not looking at the graffiti on my door, but I couldn't resist spitting on the Walrus's door.

Outside, it was a beautiful fall morning, and as soon as the sun hit my face, I felt better. I even smiled. With my earbuds in, pumping my brain full of happy music, I headed down to the river valley. I wanted to go to "our spot."

Our first night together, after dancing away the night, we had only cuddled. As horny as we'd both clearly been for each other, the dancing, the drinking, on top of a long workday for both of us, had just tired us out. I fell asleep in his arms.

I woke up before Steven in the morning, and I propped myself up on one arm and lay there watching him sleep, his mouth partly open. I leaned down, and kissed his forehead. He opened his eyes. They were so green, so bright and wonderfully green. "Brunch?" he said.

He took me to the Duchess, and we ate and played a bit of footsies under the table. After brunch, I was ready to take him back to his place, rip his clothes off, and finally get naked with him, but Steven had other ideas. "I want to show you somewhere," he said, and he took me by the hand and led me to what became "our spot."

The river valley stretched out below me, now all orange and yellow, replacing the green as far as the eye could see that first day. The flowers carefully planted in boxes along the path were gone now, but that Saturday, they'd been bright bouquets of color. Steven had led me off the path though, and onto the hill, down a small worn trail through the grass. "Where are we going?" I had asked him.

"You'll see," he'd said with a smile.

About halfway down the hill, Steven had led me off the path and into the bushes. He had laughed as I'd shrieked at a passing wasp. And then we were there: seemingly in the middle of nowhere, there was a little wooden bench, with a breathtaking view of the river in both directions as it wound its way through the city.

"How did you find this?" I'd asked.

"Stumbled across it by accident," he'd replied. "I don't even know why it's here, but I like coming here when I need to breathe deep and reconnect." He took my hand. "I've never brought anyone here before."

I had kissed him then, long and firm and hard, and then we'd sat on the bench, and we'd talked about nothing, everything. I'd lain there with my head in his lap while he played with my hair and we had just talked. When we were done, I had kissed him, and thanked him for sharing his spot with me.

"Our spot now, I guess," he'd said, and he'd kissed me.

Standing there, looking at the river in autumn, I wanted him to kiss me again so badly.

Chapter 21

Dinah was already sitting down when I got to the restaurant. She rose to greet me, and after we hugged, she held me by the shoulders. "You look like hell."

"Thanks. Always what a boy likes to hear."

"Well, a hag never lies. So what happened?"

"One second." I waved our server over and ordered a gin.

"Alex, it's noon. That can't be a good sign."

"It's not." I brought Dinah up to speed. I told her about Allan accosting me in the hall, about the phone call, about the Ecstasy. I told her about the sex, again not mentioning that it had been with Aaron. I told her about the second phone call, and about Brandon punching me, and about the vandalism at my apartment. By the time I was done filling her in, our lunch had arrived, and I was finishing my second drink.

"It's crazy, Alex. I don't know what to say."

"Do I go to the cops? They already showed up at Steven's once. Chances are, they've gone back and are looking for him by now."

"Won't they contact you then?"

"Probably."

"What will you tell them?"

"What can I tell them, Dinah? It doesn't even seem real when I'm telling you."

"And you can't bring up the Caterpillar. You don't want to get involved in some big drug investigation."

"Last thing I want right now."

"Do you want me to come over and help scrub the paint off?"

"Nope. I'm leaving it."

"Alex, that's crazy. Why would you want to do that?"

"It's just words, Dinah. Words don't hurt. I won't let them hurt. What hurts is not being able to go to Steven."

"When is this guy contacting you next?"

"I have no idea. Why?"

"I want to hear him. Put him on speaker."

"What if he knows? He could hurt Steven more than he already has. More than I already have."

"He won't be mad at you, Alex."

"How could he not be?"

"Did you have a choice?"

"Maybe. I mean, how does this guy know what I'm doing? Does he have cameras everywhere? I doubt it. It's too personal to be that high-tech. It's just someone fucking with me, and I can't think of anyone who would hate me this much, but I could have lied. I could have tried at least."

"You can't know what he's capable of. He's clearly pretty twisted. Don't beat yourself up." I finished my drink and went to wave the server over. "And stop drinking. That won't help."

"Thanks for the advice."

I ordered another drink. Dinah shook her head at me. My phone vibrated on the table.

"Is that him?"

"It's Brandon."

"You should fix that, too."

"Fix what? That one, I'm completely innocent on. This kid is psycho clearly."

"One psycho at a time?"

"That's how I like to keep it."

"What did he say?"

"Just telling me not to come out tonight."

"Well that I can agree with!"

"Har dee har har. I'm meeting the twins for wings. I'm not planning on going clubbing."

"Unless you're forced to."

"I'm not enjoying this, Dinah."

"I know, Alex, it's just . . ."

"Just what?"

"He didn't really make you do anything you might not normally do."

"I wouldn't ever cheat on Steven."

"But you didn't. Because you didn't have a choice. And Friday, you guys were broken up."

"What are you saying?"

"Think about it, Alex. He gave you a free pass. Some people could see that as a good thing."

"I'm not one of those people."

"I know you're not. But think about it. He has to have a motive. What could it be?"

That was a good question and I had no idea. Once I could figure it out, maybe I would be one step closer to getting Steven back.

Chapter 22

It had only been six months. I hadn't met everyone in Steven's life, probably. Well, I'd met everyone important. His mom lived upstate, his dad had passed away. His sister and her second husband had a brood of kids. He wasn't really friends with anyone at work, but I'd met them all anyway, his boss, his colleagues, Ugly Angie who answered the phones. There was nothing there, nothing that would make someone do something like this.

Steven was well off, but far from rich, and it didn't seem to be about money anyway. It was about sex, and sex made it personal. But in our personal lives, mine or Steven's, there weren't many people we had let get close. There were Dinah and Christopher of course, the twins, Brandon, whatever boy Brandon brought along to our little outings, be they brunch or movie nights or dancing at Wonderland.

Wonderland. Was there anyone there who'd shown undue interest in Steven? He's hot, everyone showed interest, but had anyone expressed it too much? Not that I'd ever noticed, and I would have noticed. I was a bit jealous, Steven said, and he would laugh sometimes at the way I would all of a sudden pop up at his side as he talked to some random hottie at the bar, putting my arm around him to make sure he knew I was there, to make sure the stranger knew that I was there, that I was his.

That was funny to think of, me being jealously possessive over Steven. The twins. Aaron. What was I doing? Dinah was right, I had gone from wanting to propose to a threeway with Wonderland's wonder twins awfully fast. Of course, to Dinah, the whole thing was awfully fast.

"Six months," she had said. "You've been together for six months."

"I know, but it feels right."

"It sounds ridiculous. Just because gay marriage is legal now doesn't mean you have to run out and get gay married."

Was that it? No. Sure, Aaron and I would have been married if we'd been able to, because that's what you do in your mid-twenties when you've been with someone that long. You get married. And that's what I wanted. A white-picket-fence fantasy of domestic bliss. Maybe that would quiet the voice in my head, the one I ignored as much as I could. The one that questioned if everything was too good to be true, the one that thought I didn't deserve the fairy tale. The one that thought that faggots didn't deserve those kind of happy endings. Taylor's voice.

"No," I had told her. "It's not ridiculous. It's romantic. And Steven will say yes, and it's going to be amazing. You'll see, Dinah. I'm going to get the ring today."

And I had. I'd gotten the ring. And the more I thought about that ring in my pocket, the heavier it felt. And then I thought I was turning thirty, and that was a heavy thought too. And that's how I had ended up at Wonderland for a drink, and that's how I had ended up talking to the Caterpillar, and that's how I had ended up coked-up with Sean Cody.

And the next day, that was how Steven found the drugs, and that led to the fight, which had led us here, and I had no idea where he was or who could have taken him. I just knew I had to find him, had to show him that I meant what the ring meant, that we were ready for our happy ending, and that I was ready to really put all that behind me.

So who could have him, and whoever it was, why would they want me to go to a bathhouse and fuck? And of all people, why did it have to be Aaron? Why didn't I try to lie first? Why did I get high and let him fuck me? Well, I wasn't even high. That's the part that was sticking in my head. The E had worn off when he looked at me with that look, when he talked in that voice. It wasn't even about doing what some crazy guy on the phone told me. It wasn't about Steven.

It was about being naked with Aaron, and what did that mean about the ring in my pocket?

Chapter 23

I went home after lunch, and when I got there, the building's resident manager/landlord was standing outside my door.

"What's this then?" he asked me, pointing toward the writing.

"I have no clue, Mr. Carroll. I came home last night and found it."

"And I got a phone call today from your neighbor about noise again."

"You know the Walrus complains about anything."

He tried not to smile, but it crept up anyway. "Mr. Carpenter," he said, emphasizing the name, "does get a little particular at times, but clearly, there's some problem going on."

"Well, I've never hid the fact I'm gay."

"And I don't care. What do the kids say these days? Haters gonna hate? I'll get this paint off your door. But has there been anything else? Anything I need to know about?"

"Nothing I can think of."

"Well, if something else happens, you let me know." He turned to walk away.

"Hey, Mr. Carroll," I called after him. "We don't have security cameras on the front door, do we?"

"No. Why?"

"Just curious."

He raised an eyebrow at me. "If you're sure."

I unlocked my apartment door. On the floor, underneath the door, was a piece of paper. It was another flyer for the Queen of Hearts show coming up on Friday. I looked at the back. Someone had written "you're invited." I threw it out.

I wasn't in the mood for drag shows. Not even the Queen of Hearts. She'd started performing at Wonderland in the summer, and taken the city's scene by storm. She was statuesque, flawless, and mysterious. She'd sashay into the club, do a number, maybe two, often with sexy backup (or in the case of the weekend before, sketchy backup like Allan), and then she'd be gone. All she ever went by was the Queen of Hearts, no other name, and no one ever saw her out of drag.

I remembered the first time I'd seen her. Steven and I had been together for about a month, and it was one of those pre-Pride parties that are supposed to start building up excitement and promoting all the actual Pride parties coming up. It was a little early, we'd thought, only late April, but what the hell! The twins had scored us all VIP passes and so away we'd gone.

"I think they got their parties confused," Steven had said as we walked down the stairs and were met by what could only be called a Valentine's party. Shimmering red hearts of all sizes descended from the ceiling, twirling on silver string. "What is this party again?"

Jesse looked at the passes in his hand. "They just say drag show. Look." He handed them to us. They were a simple flyer, two fierce eyes, wide and made up, with lightning bolts for irises.

"Well, let's grab a table close, and see what all the fuss is."

Wonderland was more a dance club than a show bar normally, and I was pretty excited to see a show. Aaron and I used to go to the drag shows every long weekend back home, and this was my first one since I'd moved. There may have been a few queens out and about at Pride the year before but that weekend was a gin-soaked blur and didn't count.

Brandon was serving on the floor, all shiny black shorts that hugged his delicious ass, and a three of hearts playing card painted on his torso, the bottom of the heart pointed down, across his six-pack and to the bulge of his crotch.

"Got it memorized yet?" Colton asked me, and I jerked my gaze away, immediately glancing guiltily at Steven, who laughed.

"Stare away," he said. "It's healthy to look. Just as long as you're coming home with me."

"Oh I am," I said, and kissed him in a way that left no doubt.

"You guys could always take him home to share," Jesse said. "He's fun."

"You've had him?"

"A couple times. When he first started here."

"Well, no thanks, guys," Steven said, and I nodded along with him, "we don't need that to keep it fun in the bedroom."

"Yet," Jesse said with a wink. "You've only been together a month. I bet you haven't even tied each other up yet."

I choked on my drink. Jesse and Colton didn't really believe in anything private, and I still wasn't used to it.

"Or maybe you have," he added, grinning. I felt my face flush and felt Steven kick me under the table. We'd only tried it once.

A thunderous overture began to play, putting an end to the conversation. The room went dark, and I felt a hand on my crotch. "Steven?" I whispered.

"Nope!" Jesse laughed, pulling his hand away.

Lights exploded onto the stage, onto four shirtless dancers standing there, hearts painted onto their bodies. The music picked up speed, and fog began to spill across the stage, and from overhead, a spotlight began to dance along the sparkling red-and-silver mylar backdrop. And then she emerged from the fog, a vision in red sequins, black hair, white skin, and legs for days! She sang then, live, a song that was both heartbreaking and sensual. I was captivated.

After the opening number, which ended with the queen being carried by her dancers, she grabbed her microphone and stepped out into the audience.

"Ladies and gentlemen, and gentlemen who are ladies, welcome to my debut! I am the Queen of Hearts, all hearts, even the broken ones. Tell me, are there any broken hearts out there tonight?" There were a few cheers. "Tell me," she said to a man cheering in the front row, "How did your heart break?"

He told some sob story about a cheating boyfriend, and she made some joke, and everyone laughed. Then she went to the next table, and the next. And then segued into a dancier song that involved a glitter cannon exploding all over the stage. As the glitter fell, she grabbed her microphone and said, "Let's talk about happy hearts now. Who here is madly in love?"

"Oh, these two right here!" Jesse yelled out, pointing down at Steven and me.

"And such a handsome couple they are!" she said. "Tell me, what's your name?" She stuck her microphone in Steven's face.

"Steven," he said, grinning, blushing.

"And who's this?" She placed her hand on my shoulder.

"That's my boyfriend, Alex."

"And how long have you been together?"

"A month."

"Oh, just newlyweds! And tell me, Alex, is this a love match?"

My face was on fire, but I didn't hesitate. "Oh yes!"

"Well isn't that wonderful! We love to see happy endings here. Speaking of happy endings," she said, and she segued into another dance number.

Steven squeezed my hand. "I love you, crazy."

It was the first time either of us had said it. And I didn't think twice about saying it back. "I love you, too." As we kissed, I saw the Queen of Hearts smiling down on us.

Chapter 24

I grabbed the flyer from the trash and stuck it to the fridge with a magnet that held a picture of Steven and me on the beach, thinking maybe I would go. Maybe we both could go.

"Wait a minute!" It suddenly occurred to me that this might not just be the club randomly flyering the gayborhood. What if this was the psycho? His first note had been on a similar flyer. But he hadn't called telling me to expect mail.

My phone vibrated, but it was just another text from Brandon. He was not letting it go. I was fed up with these random "you're a slut" texts, so I figured, if he wasn't going to believe me, I might as well let him have it.

And he tasted great! I texted back, turning my phone off.

I turned on the TV and stared at it until it was time to leave for wings. When I turned the phone back on, it went mad with missed messages, furious and scathing and almost unreadable texts from Brandon. I read them and laughed as I walked to my car. I started backing out, and it *KLUMPed*.

"What the hell now?" I said, getting out. My rear passenger tire was flat, slashed. "For fuck sake!" I kicked the car.

I called a cab, and while waiting for it outside the building, I debated who would have slashed the tire. I guessed it was the same guy who'd graffitied my door. The way I saw it, it was either the psycho kidnapper or the psycho twink. I didn't know how Allan would've known where I lived, though. Brandon wouldn't have done it, would he have? No, he couldn't have. He was working when my door got graffitied, and anyway, he just wouldn't have. Yes, he was fuming mad, and yes, I'd made it worse with my text, but he wasn't a nut job, was he?

I didn't really know. I'd only met him that year, the same time I'd met Jesse and Colton and Steven. Before then, it really had just been me and Dinah, and occasionally Twitten after they'd started dating. I was enjoying my solitude in my post-Aaron world. Until Steven. Everything had changed when I met Steven.

A yellow cab pulled up, and I gave the address, texting the twins that I was on my way.

Just like weekend brunches at the Duchess, Wingsanity Wednesdays at the Peppery Pig were tradition for us. A tradition I could only hope Brandon and Psycho Boy were going to skip. It was packed when I got there, the wing special, the draft specials, the free pool all combining to form an irresistible Wednesday night combination. I saw Jesse waving at me and headed for them through the throng.

"What is going on?" Jesse said as I sat down. "Pour yourself some beer, bitch, and spill."

I helped myself to a glass of beer, and we toasted. "What have you heard?" I asked.

"Brandon has been in a state, and we heard you got in a fistfight with him at the bar?"

"Hardly a fistfight. He slugged me a couple times."

Colton took my chin in his hand and looked at my eye. "He got you good. What did you do?"

"Did you actually jump his boyfriend at the tubs?"

"I ran into Allan there, and he attacked me, thinking I was going to tell Brandon, and then later, told Brandon I hit on him. That's all."

"He tasted good?" Jesse asked with a smirk.

"That was just me fucking with Brandon. And he didn't waste any time telling you that, did he?"

"More importantly, what were you doing at White Night?"

"Yah, we thought you weren't going."

I did a quick tally of pros and cons in my head, and decided that I needed some advice on what to do next anyway. Over wings (the house special hottiyaki flavor), I filled them in on everything: the phone calls, the flyers, the sex. Jesse of course wanted every detail.

"Who was he? Was he hung? Was he good? How many times did you cum?"

"For Christ's sake, Jesse, that's not really the point of the story."

"But it's the good part. Colton, remember when we used to go to White Night and put on a show in the sling? We should do that again."

"Down boy," Colton replied. "Alex, this has gone too far. You have no idea who'd want to do this to you? No one that hates you?"

"Not like this. You should have heard the vitriol in his voice . . ."

"Oooh. Vitriol. Good vocab."

"Thanks, Jesse. He absolutely loathed me. When he called me faggot . . ." I paused.

"What is it?" they asked in twinly unison.

"I just thought of someone who hates me, hates all gays."

We looked each other in the eyes and said as one, "The Walrus!"

Chapter 25

It had to be him! He fit the profile, the gay-hating crazy loner. Why hadn't I thought of it before? And it made sense, that'd he'd want proof that gay people were just like religious nuts said: partying whores incapable of a real and loving relationship!

"Will you guys come with me?"

"Wouldn't miss it for the world!" Jesse said, even as Colton asked, "Are you sure you shouldn't just go to the police now?"

"Not until I get Steven out! To think, all this time, he's just been across the hall!"

"Now Alex, you don't know that."

"It has to be. Are you coming?"

Jesse slammed back his beer and jumped to his feet. "Super gay power, activate! Away!" We tossed some money down for our bill, including a huge tip for our waiter (whose basket was far more appetizing than the basket of wings when it came right down to it), and we were off.

"You might as well tell us about the guy you did," Jesse said. "It might not mean anything but it will pass the time." We piled into Colton's car.

"Can you guys keep a secret?"

"Of course!" they said as one.

"I used to date him."

"You hooked up with an ex? Dude!"

"Jesse, you're not a surfer, you don't have to dude all the time."

"It's part of what makes me sexy."

"That's not what makes you sexy," Colton said, reaching his hand in between Jesse's legs.

"Stop it, you two."

"Making you horny?"

"Always, but no more sex unless it's with Steven."

"So an ex?"

"My ex, Aaron. From back home."

"Weren't you guys together forever?"

"Six years."

"Was it weird?"

"No, it was . . . nice."

"Why'd you break up again?"

"It wasn't going anywhere. We were in a rut."

"Well, he was in your rut anyway."

"You're a pig, Jesse. He gave me his number. He says he's here all week."

"Are you going to call?"

"I kinda have a lot going on."

"Bring him to the bar tomorrow."

"What's at the bar tomorrow?"

"Go-go boys and cheap shots, duh. It's Thursday."

"How do you stay so good-looking going out all the time?"

"Cum is good for wrinkles."

"You're a pig, Jesse."

"A pig with a wrinkle-free ass."

We laughed as Colton pulled up to my building. "What exactly is your plan here, Alex? We can't just ask him if he's a sociopath."

"And we can't break his door down and see if Steven is there." Jesse paused. "Can we? Oh please, can we?"

"No, we're going to wait until he leaves, and then go in and look around."

"How are you planning on getting into his place?"

"That's where you come in." I smiled at Jesse. "I hope you're feeling flirty."

"Always! Who do I need to flirt with?"

"My landlord."

Chapter 26

"So a few weeks ago, I had left my keys at Steven's, and had to buzz Mr. C to get in. He has a rack of keys in his hall for every unit. Jesse, you flirt, while I steal the Walrus's keys."

"What about me?" Colton asked.

"Here's my key," I said, handing it over. "Perch yourself at my peephole and keep watch."

"Why does Jesse get to be the flirter?" We both looked at him. "Okay, fine. No doing anything without me, though!"

"We're not seducing him, Colton, just flirting."

"I know my boyfriend," Colton replied. "And you've had quite the week too. Us, your ex, Allan." He stuck his tongue out at me. "Which reminds me, Brandon hasn't texted us in at least an hour."

"Thank God," I said. "Okay guys, we ready?" They nodded.

Jesse and I got out on the second floor, while Colton continued up to mine. "What's the reason we're going there anyway?" Jesse asked.

"Simple, I'm just going to tell him about my tire. It's perfect. It's a legitimate reason to get us in the door, then I'll ask to use the bathroom, and you keep him busy."

"Is he even gay?"

"Does it matter?"

"Maybe for another night," Jesse said with a wink. "He's a handyman. And you know how I love getting hammered and nailed."

"Do you ever not think with your dick?"

"It's the biggest brain I have, babe."

We were nearing Mr. Carroll's. "Shut up." I knocked on the door.

"Who is it?" he called from inside.

"It's Alex, from 14C."

He opened the door. "What's up?"

"You know how you said to come talk if there's any more problems? Well, I have one."

"Come on in."

"This is my friend Jesse. Jesse, Mr. Carroll."

Mr. C ushered us into his living room. "Can I get you boys a drink?"

"I'm good, thanks," I said, even as Jesse piped up, "a beer would be great, thanks." I could tell by the look in his eyes he was already planning on bringing Colton down to get their plumbing checked. He was hot, I guessed, for an older guy. No Alex, focus, I told myself.

Mr. C came back from the kitchen with a couple of beers, gave one to Jesse, cracked one himself. "So what's up, Alex from 14C?"

I told him about my tire being slashed, I told him about the weird guy on the intercom. I didn't tell him about my window because I figured that would spook him too much, and he'd just call the cops. I couldn't help but notice that Mr. C kept his eyes on Jesse pretty much the entire time I was talking, and that Jesse was doing his show-off-my-muscles stretch, not to mention sitting there with his legs spread just enough to give a great package view.

"Can I use your bathroom?" I asked.

"Wha . . . Sure . . ."

I glanced back over my shoulder as I went down the hallway. Jesse was at the window. "It's a great view." It wasn't. We were on the second floor.

"Yeah, I'm loving the view myself," I heard Mr. C say. Men!

There was the key rack. I scanned it quickly, found the spare keys for the Walrus's apartment, and then ducked into the bathroom and flushed. Tucking the key in my pocket, I went back down to the living room, where Jesse was bent over on all fours examining Mr. C's DVD collection.

"I can't believe you have every *Star Trek* episode ever," he was saying.

"Anyway thanks for your time, Mr. C," I said. "I don't want to keep you, but I just wanted to let you know."

Jesse stood up, stretching his arms above his head, showing a bit of abs and belly button. Even I was distracted.

"You guys don't have to leave. We can hang, have a couple beers."

"Maybe another time." I grabbed Jesse's hand.

"Yeah, maybe another time. I really wanna see the tribbles DS9 one again."

"Anytime," Mr. Carroll said, showing us to the door. When Jesse leaned over to tie his shoes, the stare was obvious, and I could tell Mr. C's pants were tighter than normal. It paid having such hot friends.

In the hall, I whispered to Jesse, "Really? Tribbles?"

"What? I'm a Trekkie. Don't judge."

"Boldly blowing what no one has blown before?" I asked, pressing the button for the elevator.

"I'll tell you this," Jesse said as we got in, "I'd rock his galaxy."

"Maybe later." I held up the key. "For now, we're busy."

The elevator whisked us up, to the Walrus and hopefully to Steven.

Chapter 27

There was only the faintest hint of FAGGOT WHORE still painted on my door. I would definitely have to thank Mr. C, maybe when I snuck the key back down. Or, on second thought, I could let Jesse do the thanking for me. My door was paint-free but locked. I banged on it. "Colton, it's us, let us in."

"Password?"

"What? Open the door."

"Not unless you know the password. Good spies always have a password."

"I'm not in the mood, Colton."

Colton made a buzzer noise. "Try again."

"Colton, I am going to kick your ass."

"Was that kick or lick?"

"Let us in."

He opened the door, laughing. "You're no fun, Alex."

"Sorry, I'm kinda distracted now, and I already have Boy Wonder here setting up *Star Wars* dates with my landlord."

"Star Trek."

"Whatever. Have you seen him?"

"No," Colton said. "But didn't you say he hardly ever leaves?"

"Do you have any better ideas?"

"Well, one. What if we pull the fire alarm?"

"Colton! That's against the law, and it's dangerous."

"Breaking into someone's apartment isn't exactly legal and easy."

"Let's just try it my way first."

"You really are no fun."

"Who gets the first peephole shift?" Jesse asked.

"You asked, you go," I said. "I'm going to take a nap."

"Really?"

"I'm exhausted, you guys have no idea. Do you mind?"

"We'll keep ourselves amused." They winked at each other.

"Just keep it down and keep your eye on his door. I don't care what you do other than that." Jesse put his eye up to the peephole, and Colton dropped to his knees. "Wait till I go to bed at least?" I said.

They laughed, and I shook my head at them, and crawled into bed. Griffin hopped up next to me, purring loudly as he rubbed up into my hand. "I miss him too," I said.

As nervous as I was, it didn't take me long to fall asleep.

Steven was on the bench at our spot. "I miss you," he said, not facing me.

"I miss you too, you have no idea."

"Do you? Why Aaron?"

"I didn't know at first. I was high."

"Do you still love him?"

"No not at all! I only love you! Well, of course I still love him, we were together for six years. But I'm not in love with him anymore."

Steven walked down the steps of the big Aztec pyramid in front of us. He stuck his hand back toward me and I raced to grab it. We walked down, hand in hand. "Are you okay?"

"Been better."

"We're trying to find you. Trying hard."

"Try harder, Alex. I need you."

"I need you too." I pulled him to me, but just as our lips met, he turned to dust in my hands.

"Try again." I turned around. It was Aaron.

"What are you doing here?"

"Helping you. You always needed my help."

"That's not true."

"Alex." It was Colton's voice. "Wake up."

"Smack him with your dick."

"Shut up, Jesse."

"Try harder, Alex," Aaron said, and then faded away.

I woke up to Colton shaking me. "What is it?"

"He left."

I jumped out of bed, suddenly wide awake. "What time is it?"

"It's almost midnight."

"You shouldn't have let me sleep so long."

"We . . . got distracted. But the point is, he left."

"Where could he be going in the middle of the night?"

"Who knows, but we gotta move fast. Who knows when he might be back."

Chapter 28

I let us into the Walrus's apartment. It was tidy, not the mess of pizza boxes and Mountain Dew cans that I was expecting. It was almost normal.

"Steven!" I called out.

"Alex! Shut up! What if someone else is here?"

"I have never seen him have people over."

"Guys, come here." Jesse was standing in the Walrus's bedroom doorway. I took one look, and thought "so much for normal." There was porn everywhere: piles of magazines next to the bed, piles of DVDs next to the TV, porn even playing on the TV. The room stank of cum. What's more, it was all gay porn. Everywhere I looked, it was cocks and ass and dildos. On the nightstand was one of those jumbo lubes with the squeeze nozzle, next to two Fleshjacks.

"Party at the Walrus's," Jesse said.

"I thought this guy hated gays?"

"I thought so too," I said, taking a step in. It was gross and sad. Is that all he did? Sit around jerking off?

"We better finish looking," Colton said, and I nodded. We checked the bathroom, the closets, even under the bed. But there was no Steven.

I stood there, at the window, looking out into the night. "We'll find him." Colton put his hand on my shoulder. "This was a long shot anyway, Alex, you know that."

"I hoped though."

"I know you did. We better go." We turned around. "Jesse, c'mon, let's go."

"Where are you?" I asked.

"Oh for fuck's sake, Jesse," Colton said, headed for the bedroom.

Jesse was standing there jerking off. "I haven't seen this one," he said, indicating the TV with his dick.

"Zip it up, Jesse. We need to get out of here."

"No, you need to tell me what you're doing here." We spun around to see the Walrus standing there in the doorway.

"We . . ."

"Tell me now or I'm calling the police." He set down a brown bag on the counter and picked up the phone.

"No, wait! My boyfriend is missing, and I thought . . ."

"You thought what?"

"I thought you kidnapped him."

"You thought I what?"

"Well, you were always so hateful."

"Yeah, what's with that?" Jesse asked. "You just act like a big bigot in public and then sneak back in here to watch your gay porn." He'd tucked himself back into his pants at least.

"You fags wouldn't understand."

"Look around, dude. You're one of us."

"I'm not one of you." He sneered at us. "Look at you guys, all smooth and muscled and perfect. Then look at me. You think I can go out to the bar and have people look at me like they look at you?"

"Well, everyone's pretty to someone," Colton said.

"Spare me." His eyes brimmed with tears. "I tried going out, and even tried talking to people. You wouldn't believe the things people said to me, the looks I got. I thought it would be better. I thought those names and those looks would be over. That's what they used to do to me in school. I thought you people would be more understanding."

"We're not all shallow," I said, suddenly feeling a huge sympathy for this lonely old man.

"Yes you are. I've seen you. I've watched the friends you have over. They're all young, they're all beautiful. Your boyfriend, he's gorgeous. You know it. You know you are, and you surround yourself with people like you, and there's no room in your perfect pretty world for people like me."

"Did you ever try?"

"I told you, I went to the bar . . ."

"Not the bar . . . Did you ever try being nice to me? I've lived across from you for two years, and you've been hateful since the first time we met. Why would I ever want to be your friend?"

He grabbed me by the shoulders. Jesse and Colton took a step toward us but I waved them off. There were crumbs in his moustache. "Really, Alex? Really?" He looked into my eyes. "You would've had me over for dinner, or gone for coffee with me?"

"Maybe." I didn't step back. "We'll never know now."

The Walrus stepped away. "Get out of my apartment."

"Look, we're sorry. Just because people are gay doesn't make them nice or understanding."

"Just go, Alex." He pointed toward the door. "I'm sorry about your boyfriend."

Colton and I stepped toward the door. "Jesse?"

"You guys go. I'll be right there."

I raised my eyebrow at Colton, who shrugged. We stepped out into the hall. Jesse shut the door behind us.

The fuck? He wouldn't, would he?

Chapter 29

Colton and I sat down on my couch. "What is Jesse doing?" I asked. "And what am I going to do now?"

"I don't know," he said. "To either."

I checked my phone, but was disappointed. Why wouldn't he have called back? What was going on? All I saw was the long list of texts from Brandon.

Suddenly I felt a wave of guilt. Maybe we were too mean to each other. I texted Brandon: **look, nothing happened between me and Allan. I never hit on him. We good?**

"Good boy," Colton said, reading the text over my shoulder.

The door opened, and in came Jesse. "What was that about?" I asked.

"I had a few things to tell him. He'll be better."

"You didn't . . ." I couldn't even say the words. Jesse only smiled.

"I did find out one thing though," Jesse said. "I know about the graffiti on your door."

"What? How?"

"Walter saw the guy do it."

"Walter, eh?"

"Do you want to know?"

"Tell us."

"He said it was around nine-thirty."

"Really? I would've just left."

"That's what he said. He seemed pretty confident."

"Who was it?"

"No one he'd seen before, but from the description, it was the same guy we saw leaving on Sunday."

"The intercom guy?"

"Yeah."

"What did he look like again?"

"He was tall, late twenties, blond hair, good-looking," Colton said.

"Nice ass," Jesse added. "We would've taken him home if we'd seen him at the bar."

"Totally!" Colton agreed. "But we didn't recognize him."

"Could be anyone. That's not much of a description to go on."

"Sorry, Alex." My chest felt empty. Jesse and Colton got up. "We should go. It's really late."

"Guys, wait . . ." I jumped to my feet, grabbed Jesse by the shoulder. "Would you guys mind staying over? I don't want to be alone."

Jesse grinned. "That's my boy."

"Not that," I said, smiling at his perpetual horniness. "Just warm bodies."

"Of course we'll stay," Colton said, wrapping his arm around me. "Let's go to bed."

Chapter 30

I woke up in the morning, sandwiched between the twins. It was déjà vu, minus the hangover but with the morning wood. Jesse's good-morning hand job almost proved to be too much of a temptation, but I jumped out of bed.

"Awww," Jesse said, a pout on his plump lips.

"I'm going to shower." I grinned as Jesse rolled over on top of Colton, who woke with a start. "You boys have fun."

The steam reminded me of Aaron again. Should I call him? Not for a hookup of course, just to catch up. It would keep my mind off Steven anyway, and the worry was eating me up, especially now with a day of silence from whoever was holding him hostage. What if Steven had tried to escape and been killed? Was the guy a murderer? Really, how far was it from torture and kidnapping to murder?

Was Steven still alive? He had to be. I had to call the cops. There was no choice. They'd already been by Steven's house, so it might not have been my fault. Come to think of it, who had called the cops? Steven didn't have family close by. Jesse and Colton would have told me if they had. Ditto Dinah.

Dinah. I should have told her the hook-up had been with Aaron. I'd planned to. Why didn't I? Was it just that I wanted to keep it to myself? That Aaron, showing up out of the blue like that, right there at that time, was just too much? Did part of me miss him? Dinah would've seen it in a heartbeat. I loved Steven. But did that mean I didn't love Aaron?

I hadn't left Aaron because I fell out of love. It was just that I couldn't shake the feeling that there was something more. We were missing the fireworks. We used to have them, back at the beginning. They'd faded after a while, though.

But they'd been back the other night. At least during the sex. My body had reacted like it used to when he touched me: shivers and goose bumps and fever. I could feel myself reacting in the shower. I leaned against the cold tile and touched myself in the steam. I shouldn't be horny, I told myself, but the throb of my hard dick made a different argument. I jacked off, and made every effort to keep Steven's face in my head as I did. The closer I got to shooting, though, the more Aaron's face kept drifting through my mind.

Suddenly, the curtain pulled back and the twins jumped in. "Oh sorry," Jesse said, grinning lewdly. "Is this a private party?"

"Can anyone join in?" Colton asked, his grin just as lewd.

They dropped to their knees in the bathtub, both of them on me at once. I knew I should push them away, knew I should get out of the shower and not let this happen, but it was too late. I had brought myself too close. I tilted my head back, one hand on each of their heads, but in my mind, I was picturing Steven and Aaron. I came hard.

"You guys are bad influences," I said, as we toweled off. They laughed and shrugged. But I wasn't shrugging. As I looked in the mirror, inside of me, a voice was screaming, *Now what was that? Why? Why did you do that? How was that not cheating? The love of your life is gone, and all you do is cum?*

"So what's your plan?"

"Waiting for a call."

"And in the meantime?"

"I think I'm going to call Aaron."

"Your ex?"

"The one that plowed you at the tubs?"

"Yes, that one, and as always, Jesse, elegantly put."

"Do you think it's a good idea?"

"I don't think it's a bad idea, at least. I have to do something. I'll go crazy just sitting around here, waiting, but I have no clues to go on to find Steven."

"Well, if you just want to keep busy," Jesse began, rubbing my butt.

"Stop it!" We all laughed, then got dressed.

The twins headed off to work, Jesse the studly personal trainer and Colton the sexy server and I sent Aaron a text: **hi it's Alex**

While I was waiting for a reply, I called Dinah at work. "Is he back?" she asked immediately.

"No, and I didn't hear anything all night last night."

"Well, what's up then?"

"I didn't tell you something yesterday at lunch. The guy I had sex with at White Night . . . it was Aaron."

"*Aaron* Aaron? Your ex, Aaron?"

"Yes. It just happened. He's up for work."

"How long has it been since you've seen each other?"

"Since I left. I hadn't even talked to him in over a year. He de-friended me on Facebook and everything."

"What does this mean?"

"Nothing. He wants to get together while he's in town, though."

"More sex?"

"Just dinner I think." My call waiting buzzed in. It was unknown! "Be right back!" I switched lines. "Hello?" It was staticky. "Hello? Steven?"

". . . hearts . . . tomorrow . . ."

"What? I can't hear you! The connection is bad."

". . . be there . . ."

The line went dead and, swearing, I switched back to Dinah.

"Who was it?"

"It was him!"

"Aaron?"

"No! The guy who has Steven. But the connection was bad. All I could hear was 'hearts' and 'tomorrow.' "

"What does it mean?"

"I don't know!" My phone vibrated again. It was a text from Aaron: **lunch?**

"Is that him?" Dinah asked.

"No, it's Aaron. He wants to do lunch. Should I?"

"Do you want to?"

"Well, I need to eat."

"Tell me how it goes? I need to get back to work."

"Bye, Dinah."

"And Alex . . . just be sure you know what you're doing."

"Thanks for the advice." I hung up, and texted Aaron back: **well, I do need to eat.**

Chapter 31

It was just lunch. I don't know why I was so nervous, and I don't know why I went to it in a jacket and tie. It was important for me to look good, to look happy, to look like I wasn't freaking out about the mess my life was in. My boyfriend was missing, being held hostage by a twisted little psycho, and I was cheating with what seemed to be a disturbing regularity.

Before I left the apartment, I grabbed the ring off the counter. It sat there in its velvet box, simple, gleaming, engraved. *My love, my life*. He was. He really was. This wasn't like with Aaron. I wasn't bored. Things were out of my control, and the things that were in my control, well, he was gone, and I was terrified. And the physical contact made me forget. It wasn't cheating. It was surviving. But it was Steven I loved, and in my heart, I was being true. I stuck the ring in my jacket pocket. Keeping it on me would remind me of that.

I changed the tire, trying not to get all worked up again. I got really nervous as I drove to the restaurant. Like sweaty palms nervous. Before White Night, the last time we'd seen each other had been the morning I moved out.

I had the last box of my stuff in my hands, and looked around the bedroom where we'd spent the last six years. I couldn't believe I was doing this. I was really leaving him, leaving my whole life. I was excited and terrified. The closet looked so weird, half empty. Putting the box down on the counter, I pulled his clothes across the rod. They were spread out, so the emptiness didn't look so noticeable.

It was the least I could do.

I picked up the box and turned off the bedroom light with my elbow. I walked down the hall. Aaron was on the couch, staring at the TV.

"I'm done," I said.

"I see."

"I'm just going to take this down then I'll come up for Griffin."

He stood up. "No, I'll take him down. Then you can just be gone." His voice was cold, but I could tell it was just because he was upset. I was upset too, but I knew it was the right thing. This whatever it was we had, it wasn't working anymore. That's exactly how I'd told him it was over.

"You don't have to."

"I want to." He scooped up Griffin and tucked him into the pet carrier. "You're sure?"

"Don't start, Aaron. I've thought about it enough already. It's done."

"Things weren't bad, you know."

I felt the frustration welling up. I couldn't go through this again. "Aaron . . ."

"Okay, never mind. Let's go."

We took the elevator in silence, and he walked me down to my car. I set the box in the back as he rested Griffin on the passenger seat. We stood there with the doors shut.

"Well, I guess that's that then."

He grabbed my arm. "Don't go, Alex." His lips were on mine, and I let myself savor their feel, their taste. It was one last time. It was a good-bye. I pulled away. His eyes were closed. "You still didn't feel anything?"

"I'm going, Aaron."

"Fine! Run away. Go hide in the city. You're giving up on happiness, you know. Our happiness."

I sighed and went over to the driver's side.

"Who are you, Alex? Who are you?"

I got in and drove away, and watched Aaron disappear in the rearview mirror. Griffin meowed on the seat beside me. Maybe I didn't know who I was but it was never too late to find out.

* * *

Outside the restaurant, I closed my eyes and caught my breath. What was I doing? Steven was missing and I was going for lunch with my ex?

"No," I said, "this is stupid." I started up the car and was just checking my blind spot when there was a knock on the car window. It was Aaron.

I turned the car off. There was no backing out now.

Chapter 32

I got out of the car, and we shared an awkward hug.

"I'm glad you texted," he said.

"Me too," I replied, and I realized I was.

Aaron held open the door for me, like he always used to do. Chivalry wasn't dead, just rare, he used to say. My face was warm, and I didn't know why, a combination of guilt and shyness. It was a little uncomfortable that it wasn't more uncomfortable. I should have gotten Dinah to come along. This felt too much like a date.

"You're overthinking," Aaron said, as we sat down at a table. "What about?"

"Lots going on."

"Well, quarter for your thoughts, let's catch up."

As we waited for our waiter, we talked work. Not that I had much to say, not having done anything all week. I didn't know if I should tell Aaron about Steven being missing. What would he say? And what would he read into the fact that I was out for lunch with him while my boyfriend was gone? I felt the ring box in my pocket, to remind me.

"Well look who it is." Our waiter was, of all people, Allan. I couldn't help but roll my eyes.

"You two know each other?" Aaron said.

"You could say that," Allan said. "Apparently I taste good."

"Look, we're just here to eat. We don't want any trouble," I said. "We can sit in someone else's section."

"No, it won't be a problem." I wasn't convinced of that, but he took our drink orders professionally, and I decided to chance it.

While we waited for our drinks, I told Aaron about the scene with Allan at the baths, and the ensuing drama with Brandon. When I was done, he laughed. "Oh Alex, you haven't changed."

"I really had nothing to do with it," I said defensively.

"No, but you sure attract drama, don't you? Remember that kid back home who was in love with you and wouldn't leave you alone? Every time we went out, there he was, hanging on your every word like you were Jesus or Gaga or something." We laughed. "What was his name? Jayden? Kayden?"

"Brayden," I said. "I haven't thought of him in forever! All I ever did was be nice to him when he was coming out."

"I know. I wasn't saying . . ."

"I didn't mean you were . . ."

We paused, and Allan picked that opportune moment to come take our orders. Aaron just ordered salad, and when I raised an eyebrow after Allan left, he said, "I'm eating healthier, taking care of myself now."

"I thought you'd been working out."

"Glad you noticed." He winked, and I had to change the topic. It wasn't a good idea to talk about our tubs tryst.

"Do you come up for work often then?"

"It's been a little more frequent lately." And he was off, telling me about the ins and outs of his days in advertising. I half-listened as I always had. It was a damn sight more exciting than my days at the bank, and a whole lot safer a conversation than recent events.

Allan brought our food. "Alex," he said, "can I steal you for a moment?"

Oh Lord, I thought, *so much for that.* "I'll be right back." Aaron raised his glass and grinned.

I followed Allan around the corner. "I don't want to—"

"Let me talk," he said. "I want to apologize."

"What?"

"I was high, and I freaked seeing someone I knew at the baths. I shouldn't have been there. I just didn't want you to tell Brandon you saw me there."

"But you did that yourself. I wouldn't have said anything, you know."

"I know that now. It was stupid, I panicked."

"You caused a lot of problems."

"I didn't think Brandon would hit you."

"Well, he did."

"So again, I'm really sorry. Can we be friends?"

"Look Allan, I'm sure you're a great guy, and—"

"I really like Brandon, and he says you're a great guy."

"Clearly he said this before he hit me."

"I'll fix it with him. I'll tell him everything. I'll tell him I made it up, that you never hit on me."

"Okay, well, I'm glad you're clearing it up."

"We good?" He stuck his hand out.

"Yes, we good." I didn't know if I believed him, but if it put an end to it, what was in a handshake?

"So who's this guy you're with?" Allan asked as we walked back to the table, like we were friends, like nothing had happened. "This the boyfriend?"

"No. An ex, actually."

"Oh wow." We had reached the table. "It's cool that you guys are friends. I could never be friends with an ex. Anyways, enjoy your lunch, boys." He blew us a kiss and went off to the kitchen.

I shook my head as I sat down. Aaron laughed. "What was all that about?"

"Twinks."

He laughed harder, and his laugh made me smile. "Oh, your phone rang while you were gone. I think they left a message."

I checked my missed calls. Unknown. "Shit!"

Chapter 33

There was a new voice mail. "Aaron, I'm sorry, but I have to check this message."

"Don't worry. Do what you gotta do."

Swearing under my breath, I called in. *"Not answering your phone, eh? Seems silly when your boyfriend is all tied up like he is. Guess it shows how much you really care. When I call back later, you better answer."*

I started to shake. Aaron slid into the chair next to me and wrapped his arm around me. I fell onto his shoulder.

"What's wrong?"

"Oh God, Aaron, you wouldn't even believe it if I told you. This whole week, it's been such a nightmare. It doesn't even seem real."

"Do you want to go home?"

I sniffed back some tears. "No, I need to eat. I'm starved. Let's at least eat." His hand lingered on my shoulder, just a second more than it should have, and then he went back to his chair.

"Do you want to talk about it?"

"Steven's missing."

"Your boyfriend? What do you mean missing?"

"Someone's taken him. I've been getting calls. I've heard him in the background, crying, screaming."

"Jesus, Alex. Have you called the police?"

"He said not to. He said he'd hurt him."

"But if he's hurting him anyway . . . What does he want you to do?"

"I don't know. He hasn't told me flat out."

"What has he told you?"

"Well, he's the reason I was at White Night."

"Sorry?"

"He told me to go there. He told me I had to hook up and then he made me tell Steven about it."

"And here I thought you were just swept up by my charms."

"Aaron, don't make this about you."

"Sorry, that's not what I meant. But it just seems an odd request from a kidnapper."

"That's what Dinah said."

"How is Dinah?"

"She's good. Engaged."

"Really?"

"Why the surprise?"

"Come on, Alex. She's been in love with you for a decade."

"She has not. We're just friends. We've always just been friends."

"I saw her look at you. I know that look." He stared down at his plate, pushing food around with his fork. "It was the same way I looked at you." He looked up.

"Aaron . . ."

"Sorry. I shouldn't have said that."

"I definitely can't handle a talk about 'us' right now."

"Forget I said it. What are you going to do?"

"He's calling back later. I'm going to make him tell me exactly what he wants."

"Do you want me to hang around for when he calls? I can take the day off."

"No. Thanks, but no. I need to do this by myself."

"Well, if you're sure . . ." He reached out over the table and brushed the back of my hand with his fingers. No lie, it felt good. I pulled my hand away, took a drink of water.

"Can we talk about something else?" I asked.

"Anything. You name the topic."

"How's your parents?" And we meandered through small talk, family and friends back home. At the back of my mind, constantly, were thoughts of Steven, but I pushed them back. I couldn't do anything right now, so I let Aaron distract me with funny stories about people we knew and places we used to go.

"Can I get you guys anything else?" Allan asked.

I looked at my watch. "Wow, it's been two hours! You're a bit late for work."

"Oh, they won't miss me. Should we go, though?"

"I think so. Just the check please, Allan."

"Sure thing, buddy!" He swished away.

"He's overcompensating," Aaron said.

"Just a bit," I agreed. "Look, I'm glad we did this. I . . . I've enjoyed myself."

"Me too. I hope things work out. Let me know what happens, okay?"

Allan brought the bill, and Aaron scooped it up.

"You don't have to get it," I said.

"It's the least I can do," he said, reaching into his pocket. He paused, a confused look on his face. He grabbed his jacket, checked the pockets.

"Problem?"

He laughed. "This is embarrassing. I can't seem to find my wallet. It must be at the hotel. Or the office maybe."

"It's no big deal." I took the check from his hand, and put some money down on the table.

"That's a generous tip."

"Preemptive strike. I don't want any more problems."

"Can I buy you supper tonight, to make up for it?"

"Aaron, I don't know. This was nice, believe me, but—"

"Alex, it's just supper."

I looked at him. His green eyes sparkled. "Six?"

"I'll call you with a place."

He walked me to my car. "See you tonight then?"

"Yes." We hugged. I breathed in his cologne. "Tonight."

I got in the car and drove away, refusing to look at him in the rearview mirror this time. As I drove, I took the ring out of my pocket and looked at it again. Lunch with Aaron made me miss Steven even more. "I need you back soon, Steven." I stuck the ring in the glove box.

Chapter 34

I didn't drive straight home. I turned right, turned left, no destination in mind. My phone was on the seat next to me, the ringer full volume; I would not miss another call.

I had too many thoughts in my head and needed some time away from the city. Just me and the open road, the music blaring from the stereo. I sang along at the top of my lungs, not caring if people driving by thought I was a freak.

I loved Steven and wanted to spend the rest of my life with him. Why did being with Aaron feel so good? Was it just sense memory? Was it just because Steven was missing? And why wasn't I freaking out more? Did that make me a bad person? If it didn't, my little sexcapades with the twins did. How could I even be thinking about getting off when the love of my life was at the mercy of a lunatic, and the love of my life before him had suddenly resurfaced just to complicate things more?

I hit the highway, speeding up. I didn't get out of the city enough. When was the last time? Steven and I had gone to the mountains for the weekend. That had been such a good time! Hiking, white-water rafting, dinner by candlelight at this cute little restaurant we found, and sex, so much sex.

My phone rang. I swerved, excited, as I grabbed it. It was Brandon. I clicked it onto speaker.

"Hey."

"Hey Alex, look, I am so sorry, man. Allan told me he was lying. I was way out of line."

"Yeah, you were. I'm glad he told you."

"Can I take you for supper, make it up to you?"

"I actually have plans already."

"Pop by the club tonight? Drinks on me?"

"Yeah, that's possible."

"Have you heard from Steven?"

"It's a long story."

"Come tell me. The twins are coming out. Hatter's on the decks."

"On a Thursday?"

"Yah. Come dance. I'm really sorry man."

"I'll try." We said our good-byes and I'd no sooner hung up when it rang again. It was Dinah.

"How was lunch with Aaron?"

"It was different. You'll never guess who the waiter was."

"Matt Lauer."

"What?"

"Well, you said I'd never guess."

"Why would Matt Lauer be a waiter?"

"Tips?"

"What?"

"Who was your waiter?"

"Regis Philbin."

"What? Really?"

"No, not really. Allan."

"Who's Allan?"

"Brandon's new guy, the one from the bathhouse."

"The crazy guy?"

"One of them, anyway."

"How was that? Did he throw a drink in your face?"

"No, nothing like that. He apologized actually, and straightened everything out with Brandon."

"Well that's good. You're avoiding the lunch-with-Aaron part, though."

"Yes, I am."

"Do we need to have dinner tonight?"

"I can't. I have plans."

"With who?"

"Whom?"

"What?"

"With whom?"

"Who are you going for dinner with?"

"Aaron, but it's not a big deal."

"Not a big deal? Two meals in one day with your ex while your current is being held captive by some random?"

"Well, when you say it like that . . ."

"Are we going to that show tomorrow?"

"What show?"

"The Queen of Hearts thing, tomorrow at Wonderland."

"Dinah! The phone call this morning, that's what they meant."

"What?"

"The connection was bad. All I could hear was 'hearts' and 'tomorrow.' But that's what he meant! It must be! His notes were even on the back of the flyers for it!"

"So yes, we're going to the show?"

"I think so!"

"Okay, I'm getting back to work. Say hi to Aaron. Don't have sex."

"Funny."

"I mean it." She hung up.

That had to be it! That was the next thing I had to do: go to the show tomorrow. Why, I had no clue, but that had to be it! Why that show? Why were the notes both on flyers for it? Was it someone from the bar? Steven and I didn't have any enemies. We had our little circle of friends, and we pretty much just stayed to ourselves.

But maybe that would be it. Maybe tomorrow night, I would figure out who this guy was and what he wanted, and I would finally get Steven back.

Chapter 35

The phone rang again. "Hello, Jesse," I answered.

"Hey, are you going out tonight? Hatter's playing, we're going . . ."

"No, I haven't heard from Steven yet, thanks for asking."

"Chill, Alex, I figured if you had, you'd've called."

"Sorry, I didn't mean to snap."

"You're stressed, I get that. Dancing is the best distraction."

"Yes, I'm going out."

"Brandon's working."

"We're good actually. I ran into Allan and he fixed everything."

"Excellent! So see you tonight?"

"Yes. Jesse, why have we been hooking up?"

"What do you mean?"

"You, Colton, me, it's just been so sexual lately. It's just weird."

"Are you beating yourself up because Steven's missing?"

"Doesn't it seem like sex should be the furthest thing from my mind?"

"You're a guy. Sex is never far from your mind. And besides, the first time we hooked up, you didn't know Steven was missing."

"That almost makes it worse."

"It's just sex, Alex. It doesn't mean you're not concerned. But if it's making you feel that bad, we can stop it. I'll talk to Colton, we can stop the flirting, stop the kissing—"

"Oh come on. Flirting is fine."

"Well, where's the line, Alex?"

"We just can't do stuff. Not when I'm with Steven."

"That's fair. We'll behave tonight. Promise."

"You never behave."

"Well, we'll *try*. See you tonight?"

"See you."

"Be sure to douche."

"Jesse!"

"Sorry, couldn't resist!" He hung up.

I did a U-turn and started heading back into the city. It wasn't a relaxing drive anymore, not with everyone calling. The phone rang again, with a text from Aaron, suggesting we meet at a trattoria downtown. It was a little intimate, but the food was amazing. I'd no sooner replied than the phone rang again.

It was him!

"Hello? Look, I'm sorry I missed your call before, if there was a way I could call you—"

"I'm not that stupid. You should be around your phone. Clearly he doesn't mean that much to you."

"He does! Just tell me what I have to do to get him back."

"Wonderland tomorrow night."

"Yes! For the Queen of Hearts show. I get it. But why there? What do you want? Just tell me."

"One more day, and you'll know."

"Is Steven all right? Let me talk to him."

"I guess there's no harm in that. Oh Stevie, your supposed boyfriend wants to talk to you." I could hear rustling and shuffling and then Steven's voice. "Alex!"

"Steven? Where are you? Are you okay?"

"Yes I'm okay. I miss you. I'm so sorry. I can't believe the last thing I did was tell you I never wanted to see you again. I love you!"

"I love you too! Where are you? Who has you?"

"Okay, that's enough." Steven was gone, just like that.

"Put him back on."

"Not tonight. Maybe tomorrow. Good-bye, Alex."

"Wait! Don't hang up!" But the line was silent.

"Fuck!" I screamed out, slamming down on the gas. As the car sped along, I screamed.

Chapter 36

By the time I got through the traffic and got back home, it was nearly time to start getting ready for dinner. My appetite was pretty much gone, though. The desperation in Steven's voice had come through the phone lines and ripped out my heart. I showered, and then stood there, looking at my reflection in the steamed-up mirror. I wasn't happy with what I saw. I wasn't happy with what I'd done, and I didn't know what I was going to do.

Whatever it took to get Steven back, yes, but what about in the meantime?

I drove to the restaurant, and got us a table. It was already starting to get dark, and the candles were lit on all the tables. It was a little more intimate than I'd remembered. I wondered if Aaron knew it was so romantic, wondered if that's why he'd chosen here. Had he been hoping for over two years that there was still a chance for us?

No, he'd seemed resigned to it, and quite content just to ride this nostalgic wave for a few days. It was the timing that was throwing me, spending time with him when I was so worried about Steven. I made a vow that nothing would happen. I wouldn't even kiss him good-bye tonight. It just brought too many conflicting emotions to the surface and I wasn't capable of processing them all.

I looked up to see Aaron coming toward me. He was smiling, and he was handsome. I made a point of not getting up when he got to the table, that way there'd be no hello hug that lasted a second too long, no inappropriate inhaling of his scent. He leaned down, kissed my cheek, sat down.

"Hey," he said.

"Hey."

"Shall we get some wine?"

Wine, I figured, was a bad idea. "Sure." Now why had I said that?

Our server came, and Aaron ordered a bottle of Sauv Blanc. We made small talk, and then we perused the menu in silence, then we ordered. Then he said, "I'd like to propose a toast. To us. To reconnecting and moving forward." That seemed innocuous enough. I raised my glass, and we clinked, our eyes never leaving each other's.

"So has anything developed?"

"He called this afternoon. I have to go to this big drag thing tomorrow at Wonderland."

"A drag show?"

"I know, right? It doesn't make sense, but that's all I know. I'm really considering involving the police."

"Well, if he's going to hurt Steven, though . . ."

"That's why I haven't . . . but it's been nearly a week, Aaron."

"What could he possibly want from you at a bar for a drag show?"

"Your guess is as good as mine. I really have no idea. If he's at the bar, if he shows himself, I'll have backup. Jesse and Colton, Dinah and Twitten—"

"Twitten?"

"Christopher. Her fiancé. You know, I can't remember why I started calling him that. He was just a twit when we first met."

"Well, I'm glad you won't be facing it alone. Especially if he's a lunatic."

"Me too. Look, can we talk about something else? I mean, this has been consuming my thoughts now for so long, and I just want to not think about it. At least for dinner."

"Absolutely. Whatever you want, Alex. What are you doing after dinner?" He raised an eyebrow, but was it an invitation or just innocent? And why was I even debating that? I was not going home with Aaron.

"I'm meeting the gang at the bar. Brandon wants to buy me a few drinks to make up for the whole Allan misunderstanding, and Jesse and Colton want to go dancing."

"Sounds fun."

"Feel free to come with," I said, knowing it was a safe offer. The whole time we were together, I could count on both hands the number of times Aaron and I had gone out dancing.

"Sure! Thanks!" That was unexpected, and perhaps unfortunate, but the offer, now accepted, couldn't be taken back. "If I'm going dancing, we're going to need another bottle of wine though." He finished off his glass, and topped both of ours off. "I'm glad this isn't awkward. It's good being friends with exes, right?"

"That's what I've always wanted for us, Aaron."

"I know. I was just so hurt when you up and left."

"You really didn't see it coming? You really didn't feel that we were just in a rut?"

"I liked our rut. I was comfortable in our rut."

"You never thought that there should be more?"

"Never once. You know, sometimes, if you spend too much time looking for more, you miss out on the great thing you have."

The conversation had waded into a place I hadn't expected, but if I was going to do this right, then it was time we had the talk. Our food came, and another bottle of wine, and I told him how I'd felt so directionless, so adrift. How frustrated I would get that we would do the same thing, week in and week out, and how frustrating it had been that he had seemed so happy with it. How our sex life was as predictable as everything else.

He retaliated in kind, telling me that he'd been perfectly content with our sex life, our social life, our home life, and how disappointing it had been that I would always make him feel like that that life wasn't good enough, that he wasn't good enough. By the end of the second bottle, we'd both cried a little, and our fingers were intertwined in the middle of the table.

"So I guess we were just at cross purposes then," I said, sniffling a little, "and there was nothing we could have done."

"You could have told me all this. We could have tried something."

"Every time I tried, you would close down. You never wanted to try anything new, to do anything new. What we had was still working for you, even though it wasn't for me. That's why it had to stop. I had to change."

"Well, I'll do something new now. Let's go dancing."

I looked at my watch. "Wow, yeah, look at the time. Again." We smiled at each other, and I reached out to lift one of his curls that had fallen across his forehead. The gesture was far too intimate, so to break the moment, I asked, "Is dinner on you or did you forget your wallet again?"

"Very funny, Alex. Actually, I couldn't find it, but I grabbed cash, so yes, dinner's on me."

"Damn! I'd have ordered dessert."

"Maybe dessert can be arranged."

"Aaron, don't."

"Sorry, sorry, I won't. I know you have a new life now." He paused and smiled. "I'm glad I'm a part of it again though."

"I am too." And I was.

Chapter 37

We were both probably too drunk to drive, but we had to do something with our cars. I followed Aaron back to the hotel he was staying at, then he got in my car, and we drove to my place. The plan was to leave the car there, and then walk to the club so we wouldn't have to deal with driving after a few more drinks.

"Can I see your apartment?" he asked.

I couldn't think of any reason to say no, so I took him up and gave him the tour. It felt weird, too weird, and maybe a little like cheating, to have Aaron in my apartment. In fact, it felt more like cheating than the actual cheating had. There was an intimacy to showing him where I slept, where Steven and I made love. Griffin was happy to see him though.

"I missed this fur ball," Aaron said, cuddling Griffin to his face.

"You hated him."

"I know." He held him out at arm's length. "Strange what you miss when it's gone." He looked at me.

"We should go."

"Yes, we better."

As I was locking up, I was all too aware of Aaron standing beside me. From across the hall, I heard the Walrus shuffling about. It reminded me to ask Jesse what they'd talked about, and to maybe get him a little something for not pressing charges after our B&E. I still had the spare key, too. I needed to get that back to Mr. C.

"So what's this bar like?" Aaron asked as we walked. "Same as 314?"

I couldn't help but laugh. The little gay bar back home, 314, had a dance floor that barely got used on weekends. "No, not really. This place is not the same as anywhere."

"It's just a bar, Alex."

"If you say so." I smirked, remembering the first time Steven had taken me to Wonderland. "Okay, prepare to be amazed."

Security checked our IDs and opened the door. Immediately, the Hatter's bass pumped into our faces. The stairwell was all swirling color. We rounded the corner of the staircase, and it was a sea of men.

"Holy shit!" Aaron said.

I laughed. "Told you. C'mon, let's get a drink." I took his hand and led him to the bar, where Brandon greeted me with a smile and a hug.

"I'm glad you made it down," he said. "Who's this?"

"Brandon, Aaron. Aaron, Brandon." Brandon raised an eyebrow at the name, then cracked us both beers. "Are the twins here yet?"

"They're around somewhere." He leaned across the bar to kiss my cheek. "What's with this?"

"Tell you later," I replied.

"Alex!" I was lifted up into the air from behind. Jesse spun me around, and then dropped me in front of Colton, who did the same.

"Who's this?" they asked, as I steadied myself. I did the introductions, earning some more raised eyebrows. Jesse then bought a round of shots, and we tipped them back.

"Oh, I love this song! Let's dance!" He grabbed both my and Aaron's hands and dragged us to the dance floor.

As we danced, Jesse yelled into my ear, "I didn't realize he was so hot."

"Hands off!" I said, laughing but also feeling a twinge of possessiveness.

"Hey, you said hands off you. He's fair game."

Colton was grinding into Aaron, who was looking a bit bewildered. We were in a crush of people, hands in the air, everyone singing along to the music at full blast. I caught Aaron's eye and smiled. He grinned back, and slipped away from Colton and toward me.

"I like your friends!"

"I can see that."

"Are they always so touchy?"

"Pretty much."

"Have you ever . . . you know?"

I thought about last Friday night, and then thought about Katy Perry, and then thought about the shower scene from the morning before. I stuck my tongue out at Aaron. "A gentleman doesn't kiss and tell."

"Since when are you a gentleman?"

"Shooter?"

"Sure."

We fought our way back to the bar, and slid up to the side, avoiding the lineup that was forming. Waving Brandon over, I ordered a couple more tequila shots. "Drink me!" We licked the salt, downed the shot, sucked the lime, then did it again.

The twins joined us for more shots, and we talked and laughed and drank and danced and laughed and drank. I couldn't think of another time that Aaron and I had actually had fun out at a club together, and told him that. He winked and said, "I told you, anything can change," and then he went off to dance with the twins while I nursed my beer.

Allan slid past me and gave me a hug. "Glad you made it. Can I get you another drink?" Had Allan bought a round? I couldn't remember. My face was on fire, and the room was blurring. This wasn't right. What was wrong with me?

I was spinning already. "I'm good right now. A little bombed actually."

He leaned in close. "Want a little something to wake you up?" He sniffed suggestively. I didn't. It was a bad idea. It was the cause of so many of my problems. But it was like the room was pulling away from me! How drunk was I? "Why the hell not?" It could only sober me up, and that couldn't be bad.

The boys were dancing. I followed Allan into the bathroom, bracing myself against the walls. The lights were painful. Allan checked his hair as we waited for an available stall. As soon as a door opened, we slid in, locking it behind us. I slumped against the metal stall. Allan's face was surrounded by a halo of light. He dumped some coke out onto his hand and lifted it to my face. "C'mon," he said. "Sniff." He took my face with one hand, pulled it toward his other hand. His skin was soft and his eyes were blue and the coke burned through me. I let out a small moan. He smiled and then treated himself.

"Thanks," I said, closing my eyes and savoring the freshness of the high. I tried to catch my breath, but it caught in my chest. What was wrong with me?

"You're welcome." And he kissed me. I pulled back.

"What are you doing?"

"I figured why not? Brandon wants to take you home with us some night. Might as well get a sneak peek." His hand was on my jeans, undoing the button.

"Allan, stop, we can't do this." I tried to slap his hand away and missed.

"Sure we can." His hand wrapped around my dick, and I was instantly hard.

"No, we can't." I pulled his hand out, regrettably. He was cute, and I was drunk, but I couldn't. There was disappointment in his baby blues. "You're cute, but with everything going on, we just can't."

"Well, don't make a big deal out of it. I was just offering!"

"Don't get pissy!" Really? He was going to blow up again?

"Don't tell Brandon about this." He grabbed my crotch through the jeans and squeezed. "I'll rip your fucking nuts off." He stormed out of the stall.

What a fucking nut job, I thought, and left the stall, to be replaced by two more twinks, giggling as they locked the door behind them. I splashed some water on my face. The coke was working and the room was slower now. I went out to find Aaron and the twins.

Chapter 38

Allan was leaning at the bar glaring at me but Brandon smiled so I assumed Allan hadn't made up some story. Yet. I scanned the bar for the guys, and saw them in a chain on the dance floor. The twins had their shirts off, of course, but Aaron's was half undone. Jesse and Colton had him sandwiched between them. I felt my lips tighten, my eyes squint.

Was I actually jealous? *It's just a dance,* I thought. *They're just dancing.* So what if their heads were thrown back in wild abandon, and so what if each bump and grind was a little deeper than it should have been? It was just dancing.

Or was it? As I watched, I felt the green-eyed monster clawing at me. I'd thought those feelings long gone, hadn't thought I could still get crazy over-the-top dramatically jealous like this anymore. But here I was, watching them dance, my ex-lover and two friends, and I wanted to smash and crash and yell out: *HE'S MINE.*

I ordered a drink and tipped it back, then ordered another. I tried not to stare at them on the dance floor, but couldn't help it. I tried to think about Steven, but my thoughts kept going back to the trio. I'd been in that scenario just last week. I knew how it ended, and when I pictured the three of them, naked, touching, sweating, I realized I was definitely jealous. I had always though of jealousy as the paranoid raging of a guilty heart, and I had lots to feel guilty about.

Had everything going on reawakened feelings for Aaron? Or was

I just drunk and a bit high and horny? If it was just horny, then why had I pushed Allan away? There he was, leaning against the bar, and talking to some guys I didn't know. He was cute, and Brandon was definitely hot, but why did my eyes keep going back to where Jesse and Colton were both nuzzling my ex-boyfriend's neck?

And why was I even at a stupid bar drinking with stupid homos when Steven was missing? I slammed down my empty glass. Brandon saw, and came over. "Need another?"

"No, I'm leaving!"

"Whoa, whoa, what's wrong?" He hopped over the bar, at least not to punch me this time. "What's going on?" He wrapped his arm around my shoulders.

"I shouldn't be here with Steven gone. It's not right."

"You can't do anything about it, Alex. Let me get you another drink."

"No, I need to go."

"You're not leaving, are you?" It was Aaron, sidling up beside us. He put his hand on my shoulder. "Let's have a drink."

"Aaron, I need to go home."

"What's going on?" Brandon climbed back over the bar and grabbed us drinks.

"This isn't good. Steven's missing, and I'm out at the bar. Again."

"What else are you supposed to do? Sit home and freak out?"

"Yes! Exactly."

"How will that help?"

"How is this helping?"

"How is it hurting?"

"Oh, it's hurting." I slammed back the drink. "Why don't you go dance again?"

"What? Are you mad I'm dancing? You invited me to come. You always wanted us to go dancing."

"There is no us, Aaron."

"I know that."

"Yeah, I can see that."

"Are you jealous?"

"No, don't be dumb. Maybe, I don't know."

"I'd much rather be bumping and grinding with you," he said, and moved in close.

"Aaron, don't."

"Is it that bad?"

"Yes. No. It's confusing."

"Hey guys! Why so serious?" Jesse and Colton jumped up, throwing their arms around us. "No heavy talk. It's boys' night."

"It's not heavy. It's all good," I said, knowing how insincere I sounded. "Shots?"

We had another round, then another, and then I didn't care. It was blurry, and the music flowed through me, and we were dancing. Jesse was behind me, lifting up my shirt, and I let him. Next to us, Colton had his lips on Aaron's nipple. Aaron reached out, his fingers finding my belt, and he pulled me toward him, and I pulled Jesse behind me. Jesse's lips were on my ear, Aaron's lips were on my neck. There were six hands on me.

I looked out from the crush of bodies and saw Allan sneering at me. He was sitting on the bar next to the cash register. He whispered something at Brandon and Brandon glared at me from across the bar. Then Aaron pulled my face down to his. I was hard and happy and nothing else mattered.

Chapter 39

I was dreaming. It was a wonderful dream. Steven and I were at our spot, and the sky was filled with stars. I was lying on a blanket, and he was propped up on his elbow. I looked up into his eyes, and they were big and brown and beautiful. He leaned down and kissed me. "I love you," he said.

I was on my back, and Colton was to my right and Jesse was to my left, and Aaron was above me, inside me. There were too many lips on me, too many hands on me. I couldn't focus. He pushed my legs down, pushed in deeper. He nibbled on my chin, the way he'd always done. "I love you," he whispered, and then began to thrust. I bit down on his shoulder as he pushed his way deeper into me. My fingers clawed into his back, into the star tattoo on his shoulder.

We made love under the stars, hidden from the paths by the bushes. The August air was warm, and the moon was overhead, and when we were done, we still didn't stop touching each other. Our hands roamed over bodies we knew so well now, trying to find out hidden secrets about each other. We laughed, we shivered, we trembled.

Aaron pulled out and I gasped, wanting him back filling me. I didn't want to feel, just wanted to feel him. But then Colton was in me, and Aaron was in Jesse next to us, and Jesse and I kissed below, and they kissed above, and limbs were tangled, and it was savage and rough and primal, and then Colton flipped me over and pulled my hips up, and he was mounting me from behind. I saw Aaron in Jesse, and Aaron was smiling at me, and Jesse's head was thrown back in absolute ecstasy.

We were hard again, and we made love again, and then we lay there again. Our clothes were in a pile at our feet, next to the picnic basket, next to the empty bottle of wine. Steven reached down and pulled a blanket up over us. He wrapped his arms around me, and nuzzled at the spot on my neck that he knew so well. I sighed. "This has been an amazing night."

Colton and Aaron had switched again, and they were both picking up pace. Jesse's fists were a blur, one wrapped around his cock, the other around mine, slick with sweat and lube. My eyes were locked with Aaron's and I could see his face scrunch, the way it always did when he was about to cum. As he let out a groan, I shot, and Jesse did too, pushing Colton over the edge. They collapsed down onto us, a sweaty, sticky mass of flesh. Aaron's mouth found mine and I held his face tight against mine. We lay there, panting, and then Colton pulled the quilt over all four of us. He turned off the bedside lamp, and in the darkness, Aaron wrapped his arms around me, and nuzzled at the spot on my neck that he knew so well. I sighed, and fell asleep.

Chapter 40

When I woke up in the morning, I was alone in the twins' big bed. I was sore and spent and my head was pounding. I could hear talking in the living room, a bit of laughing. I flinched as I got out of bed, pulling on my jeans. The sun through the window was far too bright.

"Morning, sunshine," Jesse said. "Coffee?"

"Ugh. Please." Colton and Jesse were sitting at their kitchen island, both just in their undies. I looked around, but it was just the two of them.

"Looking for Aaron? He had to leave."

"He said to say good-bye."

I felt . . . disappointed that he hadn't said good-bye in person. Even through the hangover, I could still feel him inside me. I could feel his absence, mingled in with regret and guilt.

"So much for behaving, hey?" Jesse said, brushing his crotch against my hand as he handed me the coffee.

"Jesse, I have so much going on in my head right now, I can't deal with you being cute." I ground my hands into my forehead. He started kneading my shoulders, and it did feel good. Steven used to give me the best massages.

I jumped to my feet. "I have to go! This is crazy. I'm going to the police."

"Whoa! Are you sure that's smart?"

"It has to stop. I'm not playing this twisted little game anymore."

"If you're sure . . ."

"Do I have any choice? The longer this goes on, the more I am letting my life implode."

They both hugged me, and even though they were beautiful and in their undies, it was, for a change, entirely nonsexual. I grabbed my clothes from where they were strewn about the bedroom, and kissed the twins good-bye. As I waited for the elevator, I checked my phone.

I had one new message.

"See you tonight, Alex. You only have a few hours left. Just remember, don't do anything stupid."

I banged my head on the elevator door in frustration. I'd been ready, I'd been sure, and now doubt was mingled in with everything else. What if it would really be done? Should I wait a few more hours before jeopardizing Steven's safety? By the time I'd reached the lobby, I'd decided to hold off going to the police again.

On the walk home, I remembered I wanted to get something for the Walrus, or Walter as I guessed I should start calling him. What did you buy to apologize to the creepy loner porn addict who lived across the hall after breaking into his apartment and accusing him of kidnapping your boyfriend?

I passed by a street vendor selling flowers, and figured why not? He had probably never had a guy buy him flowers before, so it might be a nice gesture. Besides, I was nearly home, and it was on the way. I bought a bouquet of carnations. They were bright and fresh, and his apartment could definitely use the color.

In the lobby, I ran into Mr. Carroll. "Alex! Everything been okay? Any more incidents?"

"No, everything's been good, thanks for asking." I discreetly patted down my pockets looking for the Walrus's spare key.

"Who are the flowers for? Romantic night with the boyfriend?"

"Actually, they're a peace offering for the Wal . . . for Walter across the hall." There it was, in my inside pocket.

"Oh, that's nice. I ran into him last night. He mentioned you guys had come to an understanding."

"Yeah." How to get it back to him?

"That's good. Well, you take care."

He turned around, and I definitely noticed what Jesse had noticed about his muscular back and shoulders. "Hey, I think you dropped something." I bent down and came back up with the key in my hand. "Did you lose a key?"

He took it from me, looked it over. "It's one of my spares, yeah. Weird. Thanks."

"No problem." I watched him walk away, then shook my head. No more cruising, I told myself. I took the elevator up.

I knocked on the Walrus's door. Walter's door. "Who's there?"

"Hey. It's Alex. From across the hall."

"One second." I could hear shuffling. The image of what he might have been doing flashed into my head.

The door opened, and there he was. I couldn't help but give him a once-over, looking for signs that what I'd pictured happening actually had been, but luckily, I couldn't see anything. No pup tent, no wet spot.

"What do you want?"

"I'm here to apologize again for the other night."

"Oh?"

"And I brought you these." I handed him the flowers.

"Thanks," he said, taking them.

"Look, did you want to come out with us some night?"

"You don't have to do that, Alex. I don't want pity friends."

"That's not what this is. It would be cool, that's all. We're neighbors, right?"

He looked at me, his expression disbelieving. "Well, I'll think about it."

"Good! Glad to hear!" I turned to go into my apartment.

"I'm glad you've made up with the graffiti guy."

"What?" I turned back.

"The guy who spray-painted your door. Glad you guys made up."

"What do you mean?"

"Well, you brought him here last night. I just assumed you guys had worked it out?"

Last night? Who had I brought here last night? I thought. And then it came to me. "What the fuck!"

Chapter 41

I grabbed Walter by the shoulders. "This is very important. Are you telling me that the guy I brought here last night is the guy you saw spray-paint 'faggot whore' on my door?"

"Yes. You didn't know?"

"No, I didn't know. Christ!" I kicked the wall.

"Whoa, Alex, is everything okay?"

"No, Walter, everything is most certainly not fucking okay. Not fucking okay at all."

I stormed into my apartment, slamming the door behind me, and a scream started deep inside me. My fingers grabbed my hair and out it came: a howl that started at my feet and slowly rose up through my body until it burst forth from my mouth. "Aaron!"

I grabbed my lamp and smashed it against the wall. Griffin jumped off the couch and ran into the bedroom. How could he? How could I have been so stupid?

"Where is my fucking phone?" I kicked the couch, digging through my pockets. I called Aaron. It went to voice mail. "Aaron! Call me now! Right fucking now!"

Crazy! It was crazy! I couldn't believe he'd done that, and then tried to be all normal and sympathetic. He knew how I felt about that word. Why would he fuck with my head like that? No, there had to be a mistake. The Walrus had to be wrong. How could Aaron have done it? Aaron was with me at the baths, and he didn't know where I lived.

Well, he'd said he didn't anyway. Even if he had though, did he have time afterward to come here and do it? How long was I at the bar? It would have been tight, but it was possible. Maybe.

Unless he'd done it before.

Where did that thought come from? If he'd done it earlier, then it wasn't just a reaction to what happened. It was planned. And if it was planned . . .

Wallet!

The thought came to me out of the blue. I remembered Aaron saying he'd lost his wallet, and suddenly I had the image of finding a wallet at Steven's. It was a horrible realization. What if . . . no . . . he couldn't have . . . he couldn't be the one.

I grabbed my jacket and headed out. There was one way to find out. I tried calling again as I walked. "Aaron, it's Alex. It's vitally important you call me when you get this. I need to ask you something."

I was vibrating, and it felt like I was going to vomit. How could I even be thinking this was true? There was no way. It was my guilt talking. That was it, had to be it. Could Aaron have done all of it? There was only one way to find out, and I picked up the pace toward Steven's house.

As I walked, I called Jesse. "You won't believe it."

"What's up, buttercup?"

"The Walrus saw Aaron spray-paint my door."

"What? Did you talk to Aaron?"

"He's not answering. But wait, it gets worse. I think he's the one."

"The one what?"

"The one who has Steven!"

"What? Alex, you're kidding me."

"No! When we went for lunch, he said he'd lost his wallet, and I found a wallet at Steven's. I'm on my way there right now. The guy from the other night, the one you saw leaving my place, could that have been Aaron?"

"I don't know. It was dark. I don't really remember. He was blond, I think."

"But maybe not?"

"Maybe, maybe not. I really don't remember. Sorry, Alex. But you were with Aaron for six years. You'd know if he was that unstable."

"Everyone changes."

"But like that? Are you sure?"

"No, and I hope I'm wrong."

"Where are you right now? Do you want me to come?"

"No, I'm almost at Steven's. Just stay on the line."

"Okay. Wow, I can't believe he's that crazy. He was good in bed."

"Shut up, Jesse."

I turned onto Steven's block and stopped short. "I'll call you back," I said, and hung up. The front door was open. I remembered locking it. I knew I'd locked it. I started to run. Maybe Steven was home. Maybe it was over.

"Steven!" I yelled.

Chapter 42

As soon as I was inside, I knew he wasn't home. The coffee table was flipped over, cushions were everywhere. There was a bowl, normally on an end table, smashed on the floor.

I fed his fish as I walked by into the kitchen, berating myself for not having thought of it sooner. In the kitchen, cupboards and drawers were open, clutter was everywhere. The picture of us he kept on the fridge was ripped in half.

I went into his bedroom next. The bed, which I remembered making, was torn apart, blankets and pillows everywhere, the mattress sliced down the center. On the walls, all the pictures of us that hung there were smashed, none of them off its hook but the glass shattered in every frame.

I called Jesse. "His place has been ransacked."

"Is the wallet there?"

"Shit, I forgot." I went out to the living room, searched around the couch, under the couch, but couldn't find it anywhere. "No."

"Well, is anything missing? Maybe it was a random burglary."

"No, it was personal. All the pictures of us are destroyed. He was angry, whoever it was."

"Try Aaron again. It has to be a mistake."

"Okay."

"Call me."

I tried Aaron's cell again, and there was no answer, and his voice mail was full. Absentmindedly, I started putting Steven's living room back together. I sat down on the couch and debated what to do. I needed to be more proactive, I decided. No more sitting around waiting for a phone call.

I called Aaron's hotel, but when I asked at the front desk for his room, they said they had no one there with that name. Of course they didn't. Maybe his work would know how to get ahold of him. It had been almost three years but I still had his office number in my phone. It rang.

"Don't Dream It, Be It Advertising," a voice finally answered.

"Hello, I was hoping I could speak to Aaron Matthews."

"Sorry, I don't think we have anyone by that name here."

What? That was strange too. He'd said at lunch he was still with the same company. "Are you sure? This is the right place."

"I've been here seven months, and I've never met anyone by that name. Can I transfer you to someone else?"

"No thanks . . . actually, yes, is Charles Kirk still with you?"

"Why, yes, Mr. Kirk is, but he's in a meeting right now. Can I pass on a message?" I gave the receptionist my number, and he promised he'd get the message to Mr. Kirk right away. Charles Kirk was Aaron's boss, or had been anyway, and we'd met several times. He'd remember me. He'd know where Aaron was.

I started cleaning up the shambles of Steven's living room as I waited. Mr. Kirk would call me back, I'd talk to Aaron, and I'd straighten this all out. Jesse was right. It had to be a misunderstanding. Aaron couldn't have done all this. He'd never had an angry thought in his life. I watched the minutes tick by on the clock on the wall, a present to Steven from his grandmother for his twenty-first birthday.

Wait a minute, I thought, and called Steven's work. I hadn't called in to see if they were wondering where he was or what they knew. Ugly Angie answered the phone, but said Steven had called in Monday morning and taken some personal time. Maybe he'd sounded weird, but she had assumed that was because he was sick. I thanked her and hung up. His kidnapper probably had Steven call in so they wouldn't suspect anything was wrong. It had been a long shot anyway, but why hadn't I done it sooner?

There were so many things I should have done sooner, I realized, more than just checking his work and feeding his fish. I should have made sure he knew how crazy in love I was, and I should have made sure he knew I was ready to settle down, and I should have never done any stupid drugs from the stupid Caterpillar at the stupid bar.

The phone rang. "Hello?"

"Is this Alex? It's Charles Kirk."

"Oh hello, thank you for calling me back. Do you remember me?"

"Of course I do, but I'm a bit surprised to get your call. Aaron hasn't worked here in nearly a year. Is everything all right?"

A year. Well, that answered that. If Aaron had lied about work, he may have lied about everything. "Everything's fine. I'm just trying to get ahold of Aaron. We fell out of touch and it's urgent I track him down. Do you know where he's working now?"

"Sorry, I don't. When he left us, he just said he was moving to be with you. We were all quite happy that you two had decided to give it another go."

"We never did . . . and this was a year ago?"

"Near as I can remember. You say you haven't heard from him?"

"Well, not exactly, but thank you for your time, sir." I hung up. Aaron had quit his job a year ago? With the supposed intention of us getting back together? What was going on in his head and where was he? Did he have Steven? Whoever had him, the next of his "ransom demands" was coming up that night. There was nothing really to do but wait until show time.

I lay my head down on Steven's couch and let myself doze.

Chapter 43

"I've missed you," Steven said, not looking back at me.

"I miss you too."

I placed my hands on his shoulders, as he sat on the bench at our spot overlooking the river. The sun was high and bright in the sky overhead. All down the hill of the river valley were carnations, blooming in the summer sun. It was beautiful, but a little weird, since the flowers were all averaging at least a couple feet in height.

"What have you been doing?" I asked him.

"Waiting for you to rescue me. To swoop in like a white knight."

"That's romantic."

"But instead you were off at White Night. I hope it was worth it."

He stood up and shook my hands off. "Don't get mad," I said.

He started walking into a throng of people that transported us from the river valley to Wonderland. The music was so loud that my teeth were vibrating. I couldn't see him. Why was the bar filled with all these little Asian girls, all pigtails and short skirts? It was supposed to be a gay bar. We hated that so many straight girls came down. I turned, and mentioned that to Dinah.

"I know, right?" she said. "I'm even a straight girl, and I hate it. You're my fags. They can go get fags of their own."

"Where did Steven go?"

"He's over there." She pointed at the fountains, big stone fountains past the bar, all dolphins spitting water. Among them, beyond

the streams of water and the little rainbows they made, Steven was naked, Jesse and Colton holding him against the wall, each of them working over a nipple. "Hey!"

"Are you jealous?" Dinah asked.

"Very."

"How can you be? Look, Brandon's waving you over."

I followed where she pointed and saw Brandon. Allan was on his knees in front of him and Brandon's hands were on his head. Brandon saw me watching and jerked his head at me, signaling me to come over. I pushed the Asian girls out of the way and walked toward him. He pulled me closer by my shirt and stuck his tongue in my mouth. It tasted like mint.

I made out with Brandon, watching across the flowers to where Steven made out with Jesse. Colton and Dinah were dancing on the bar. Allan started undoing my belt and I didn't push him away this time. Steven glared at me.

"I thought you missed me," he yelled angrily across the bar, and the music scratched to a halt.

Everyone was silent and still. "I do miss you," I said, and I pulled up my pants from around my ankles and pulled the ring out of my pocket. I walked across the field toward him and got down on one knee.

"Oh, I'm going to cry," Dinah said.

"Will you marry me?" I handed Steven the ring.

He took it, looked at it, held it up to the mirrorball. The ring grew, the diamond on it was huge, bigger than Steven, bigger than the bar, bigger than the sun. It was too heavy for him to hold. I took it from him, but it weighed me down. I started to sink into the dirt.

"Help me!" Jesse and Colton looked at me from where they were fucking, but went back to it. Allan and Brandon were walking away from me. I was waist-deep, and couldn't pull myself out. Dinah was all in black, and she was crying, and Steven wrapped his arm around her and they walked away. "Help me you bastards!" I was in the dirt up to my armpits.

"Need a hand?" Aaron was standing above me, holding out his hand.

"Not from you!"

"Suit yourself," he said and flew off.

I kept sinking, spitting out the dirt as it filled my mouth. Then my nose, then my eyes, and then all I could see was black.

I woke up, panting, sweating. *The fuck?* I thought. I glanced at the clock on the wall. It was after six. I had three missed calls, two from Jesse, one from Colton. I tried Aaron's cell first, and it went straight to his full voice mail again. Then I called Jesse back.

"I'm coming over before we head to the club," I told him.

"Have you heard from him?"

"No. I'll be there in an hour."

"See you then."

I yawned and stretched, and looked around one last time for the wallet. Outside, the sky was already getting dark. I decided to shower and change there. Steven's stuff fit me, and I didn't want to go home. I needed to be around people as quickly as possible, people who had gin, and lots of it. I found an outfit, took it into the bathroom with me.

I stripped off, stepped into the hot shower, and furiously scrubbed up. I was just washing my hair when there was a bang on the bathroom door. "Police! Who's in there?"

Chapter 44

I froze. *Oh no. What should I do, or say?* I stuck my head out of the shower and called out. "My name is Alex Lewison. What's wrong, officer?"

"We're looking for Steven Thompson. Do you know him?"

"He's my boyfriend."

"We're going to need you to come out and talk."

"I'll be right out." What were the cops doing here? Moreover, if the person who had Steven—and I still didn't want to believe it was Aaron—saw them here, what would that mean? I frantically rinsed off the shampoo and the suds. When I turned off the water, the silence was heavy.

"Do you live here with Mr. Thompson?" one of the cops called through the door.

"No, I came to visit."

"Are you almost done in there?"

I looked at the bathroom window as I got dressed and for a second, I debated crawling through it and bolting. I decided against it though. That would be kicking a hornet's nest. The last thing I needed was cops chasing me. I just had to talk them out of the house. I opened the door, and there were two uniformed officers in the living room. Thank God I had cleaned it!

"So do you know where Mr. Thompson is?"

"Not right at the moment, no. Is there a problem, officers?"

"It was reported that he's missing."

"No, he's not missing."

"When was the last time you spoke to Mr. Thompson?"

"Just yesterday. Who reported him missing?"

The officer who was talking checked a notepad she carried. "A Mr. Brandon Sweet. Are you familiar with him?"

"Yes, I know him."

"Do you have any idea why he would have reported Mr. Thompson missing?"

"I have no clue, officer. When did he do this?"

"Sunday. We haven't been able to locate him. He hasn't been to work."

"He's been sick."

"Are you expecting him soon?"

"No, but I will be seeing him tonight."

"And where would that be at?"

"We're going to Wonderland, there's a party."

They asked for the address of the club, what time we'd be going, took my particulars. "Is there anything else?" I asked. "I really need to be somewhere."

"Is everything all right, Mr. Lewison?"

"Please, call me Alex, and yes, everything is fine. I just really need to get going."

"Would you have Mr. Thompson please get in touch with us as soon as you talk to him?"

"Absolutely." I walked toward the door, hoping they'd get the hint, pulling out my phone.

They looked around as they headed out, and I smiled like nothing was wrong, and hoped that it was believable. I watched as they got into their car and drove slowly away. As soon as the car pulled around the corner, I let out a huge sigh of relief.

Had I done the right thing, lying to them? Was that my opportunity to enlist their help? Would they show up at the club tonight, and would that help or hinder getting Steven back unharmed? Why had Brandon gone to them? That last question was at least one I could get an answer to.

I dialed his number. "What's up, Alex?" he answered.

"Brandon, did you go to the cops about Steven?"

"On the weekend, yeah, when we first found out he was missing. Before you'd told me about the call telling you not to. Why?"

"They just left Steven's."

"Did you tell them everything that was going on?"

"No, I didn't want to chance it."

"Oh, well, I hope it doesn't cause problems. I just thought someone should call."

"Well, no harm yet I guess. Look, is everything good with us?"

"Yeah, shouldn't it be?"

I didn't want to tell him about Allan in the bathroom. If Allan hadn't said anything, hadn't stirred up any more drama, I sure wasn't going to. "Just checking, babe. See you tonight." I hung up, and started over to Jesse and Colton's.

Chapter 45

As I was walking to the twins', I tried calling Aaron again. It rang once, twice, and then he picked up. "Hello?"

"Aaron! Where the fuck have you been?"

"What do you mean? I was driving home and had my phone turned off. What's up?"

"I think you know. What the fuck was the big idea? Did you think I wouldn't find out?"

"I don't know what you're talking about, Alex."

"Like fuck you don't. Someone saw you, Aaron."

"Saw me what?"

"Saw you paint my doorway."

"The graffiti? Don't be crazy, Alex. I would never do that."

"Bullshit, Aaron! Do you have Steven?"

"What? Are you kidding me?"

"No, Aaron, I'm not. You've lied about everything. I called your work, I know you quit a year ago. I know you weren't in town for work. Come clean. Now."

"Alex, it isn't what you think."

"Where are you, Aaron? Put Steven on the phone."

"I don't have your boyfriend, Alex, and frankly, I am disgusted you think I would even have it in me to do something so insane."

"My neighbor saw you graffiti my door. If you did that, who knows what else you'd do. Tell me, why the club?"

"What?"

"Why do I have to go to the club tonight to get Steven back? What's there?"

"This conversation is over, Alex. Call me to apologize when you realize how insane you sound."

"Don't you dare hang up on me . . ." I screamed into the phone but the line was dead. When I called back, of course, his phone was off. Why had he even answered? Why was he lying? What did he want? Did he think that this was the way to get me back? Was this all some elaborate plot to get me to realize how much I missed him, how much I still loved him?

There was a small whisper of doubt in my brain, telling me that it wasn't him, telling me that he couldn't have done it. He did still love me, it was obvious in how he looked at me, in how he'd fucked me. Hell, he had said it flat out the night before, although yeah, sure, he'd been drunk and about to cum.

It had to be. Everyone had been asking me who might have had cause to come after me or Steven like this, and it fit. Steven had exes too, but did he have exes who'd shown up randomly like this, with eyewitnesses to their vandalism? But then why would he have gone up with me to my apartment? And was that police car there driving ever so slowly in the street watching me?

Okay, Alex, I told myself, *you're overthinking and you're paranoid. It's nearly time to go to the club, and then not only can you have a few drinks and relax, you can figure this all out.*

I buzzed the twins, and ascended again to their condo in the clouds. Had it really only been this morning that I'd left? Had the drunken fourgy only been last night? I banged on the door, and Jesse opened it up.

"Wow guys, you look great." They always did, but they were over the top tonight, Jesse in white with a black tie, Colton in black with a white tie.

"Thanks!" they said, each squeezing one ass cheek as they pulled me inside.

I brought them up to speed, and they both again expressed their doubts that Aaron could be behind it. "I know we just met him, but he just didn't seem crazy," Colton said.

"Here's my number, call me maybe," Jesse added, earning him a punch in the shoulder.

"Really though, Alex, you're basing it all on what the Walrus saw through his peephole. And until a day ago, you'd never even had a polite conversation with him, and now you're taking his word over a guy you've known for how many years?"

"We were together for six."

"And did he give you any indication in that whole six years or in the three since that he's a deranged lunatic willing to stop at nothing to get you back?"

"I mean, don't get us wrong, you're great in bed, and clearly, that ass is worth kidnapping for but, really . . ."

They did make a kind of sense, and what's more, I really wanted to believe what they were saying. "But then who has Steven?"

"Maybe it's just some random nutcase. The city is filled with them after all. We'll be with you tonight, and if anything happens at this party, we've got your back."

"We'll get him back tonight, or we'll all go to the police tomorrow."

"Is Dinah coming tonight?"

"And Twitten."

"The whole gang."

"So what exactly is the point of this show anyway? Fundraiser?"

"The Queen of Hearts is retiring."

"Retiring? Didn't she just start this summer?"

"Yah. Came out of nowhere, what, seven months ago?" Jesse looked at Colton for confirmation.

Colton nodded. "Yeah, around then. And now she's done. Moving on to some new bar, to grace them with her divine presence."

"She's just a drag queen, guys."

"But what a queen!" they said as one, and sighed dramatically.

We laughed. It felt good to laugh. "Okay, let's go. I want to be there early, and get a good table. And then," I said, "we will see what we will see."

Chapter 46

The club was silver. Everything gleamed in candlelight from the tables set up around the dance floor-turned-stage. Silver mylar curtains sparkled along the wall. The music, normally the thumping throb of house, was a more mellow trance. The Hatter, in a silver jacket and sunglasses, waved to us as we came in.

Dinah and her fiancé were already there, sipping red wine at the bar. Christopher aka Twitten was wearing plaid. I shook my head. Plaid was so overdone, and combined with the beard and glasses, just exacerbated his hipster twittiness. Dinah was stunning, though, in a short black skirt showing off her legs. I was feeling a little underdressed to be honest, and then I realized I never thought about what people were wearing. I noticed what they weren't wearing, like Brandon behind the bar, not wearing much and looking great doing it (how *did* that boy get abs like that?).

I had tried calling Aaron a couple more times but there was nothing. My phone had never been so ominously silent. I set it on our table right in front of me, ready to pounce the second it started vibrating. If I'd had any desire to watch the show, the five of us had a great table. I wasn't thinking about drag queens, though. I was thinking about Steven, and kept looking around, hoping to see someone staring a little too hard, hoping to see someone who looked like they knew where he was.

It occurred to me, then, that Steven and I had never missed a

Queen of Hearts show. I thought of that first show, where he'd said he loved me for the first time. We had made a joke of it, that we said we loved each other at a show starring the Queen of Hearts. It was corny, like so much had been corny in our summer together. The sense of missing him was so big inside me, it made my whole body tremble. I felt the ring box through my pocket. Would he have said yes?

Of course he would have. He loved me. He'd said so, at this table, in this bar, at the first show starring . . .

The overture burst from the speakers, and I got caught up like I always did. Dinah giggled and clapped her hands; she never got out anymore, since Twitten came along. He was sitting next to her, his arms crossed, looking uncomfortable as hell. Like he had a stick up his ass, in a place where no one minded a stick up his ass.

And then there she was, the Queen of Hearts, in a gown of flowing red, a ruby-studded crown set in her black hair. She didn't walk onto the stage, she floated. She opened with a torch song, beautiful and romantic, about two separated lovers finding their way back to each other.

My phone vibrated. "Hello?" I whispered, trying to be as discreet as possible.

"Are you enjoying the show, Alex?"

"Where are you?" I scanned around the club. There were people on phones everywhere!

"Pay attention, Alex. There's someone here you know."

"Where?" The line was dead. Dammit!

"What is it?" Jesse asked.

"It was him! He says there's someone here I know."

"Other than us?"

"You're not being helpful, Jesse."

"Oh I hope my little show isn't interrupting your conversation." The Queen was standing in front of our table.

"Sorry."

"Was it something you wanted to share with the club?"

I felt my face glow. "No, we'll be quiet." The others were chuckling at my embarrassment.

"Well good, a pretty face like yours should just enjoy the night." She smiled at me, and then waltzed off across the floor to chat with another table.

"She's very graceful," Dinah said.

I hushed her. "Don't bring her back!" I kept scanning the crowd. I knew so many of them, or recognized them at least. There was the Hatter, in the booth and waiting for the Queen's signal to play the next song. There was the Caterpillar, holding court in his corner, dispensing treats to the fiending and the hurting. There was Allan, talking to Brandon at the bar. Ginger Jeff and Big Dick David and Bottom Bobby and Humpty Dumpty . . . so many guys I knew from the bar, but which one was I supposed to be looking for?

"It's the Walrus!" I nudged Jesse.

"Oh, I told him to come. I'll be right back." *The fuck?*

Jesse slid away from the table and went over to Walter, and brought him down to the table as quietly as possible as the Queen of Hearts was carried around by two backup dancers, both with swarthy good looks. Was it the Walrus? Had it really been him all along?

They watched the show but I watched the Walrus, and the rest of the crowd. Nothing seemed out of place. Everyone was glued to the numbers unfolding before us, as they built up faster and flashier. Then the Queen disappeared behind the curtain to change and we were left to watch the gyrating antics of her scantily clad dancers.

"Jesse, what did you invite him for?" I whispered.

"He needs friends. He's lonely."

"I'm still not sure about him."

"Trust me, he's harmless."

"Walter," I said louder. "Are you positive that the guy you saw painting my door was the one I brought up?"

The look on his face wasn't right. It was hesitant, and guilty, or was I just reading into it? "Yes."

My phone vibrated under my hand. When I picked it up, I could hear the music that was playing coming at me both from the speakers and through the phone. Whoever was calling was calling from inside the club. I jumped to my feet and looked around as I said, "Where are you?"

"Seen anyone unexpected yet, Alex?"

"Who is this? Where are you?"

There was a sudden quiet and a slow song began to play. I sat back down. "Where are you?" I asked again, but the line was dead. The Queen of Hearts came back out, in a different outfit, a silken shawl draped about her shoulders.

As she performed, Allan suddenly appeared on his knees at the side of the table, holding a tray of shooters. "Here, these are from Brandon," he whispered. He slid them over to Twitten and Dinah and me and then crept out onto the dance floor to deliver the rest. The Queen was parading about, her number crescendoing. Allan passed the shooters to Jesse and Colton and to Walter, and I saw him shoot Walter a look. Was it disgust? Maybe Walter had been right about how our friends would perceive him. Allan went to stand up and leave just as the Queen swept by our table.

They collided, and both came crashing to the floor. We all jumped to our feet, and the Hatter hit pause on the music. The silence was filled with scattered startled conversation. Allan stood up, helped the Queen back to her feet. Her shawl was on the ground and Colton leaned down to grab it, but before he did, I saw it on her shoulder.

A star tattoo. I knew it well.

"Aaron? What the . . . ?"

Chapter 47

She froze briefly, then swiped the shawl from Colton's fingers and wrapped it around her. How could I not have noticed it? It was so apparent now, I could see it in her (his) eyes. Behind the false black lashes, they were the same green eyes I'd gazed into for six years! The music started up again, and I watched the show, but now I noticed that she (he) kept looking at me.

"Aaron? Really?" Jesse asked.

"Dude, your ex is a hot woman," Colton said.

"I can see it too," Dinah said. "What are you going to do?"

"I have no idea. The caller said I'd see someone I knew. Is this it? Has Aaron really been living in my city and performing right before my eyes for six months now and I had no idea?"

The table behind us shushed us, and almost as one, we turned and said, "Shut up!" It was funny, or would have been if the floor hadn't just given out underneath me. I did my shot, the one Allan had brought, and then did Dinah's. "Hey!" she said, as I reached for Twitten's.

"I need this." I tipped back the shot, and the three, so quick on top of the wine we'd been drinking since the show started, sent a wave of nausea through me. Aaron doing drag? It was impossible. I flashed back to him saying how everyone changes. He'd quit his job and disappeared. To do what? To come here and do drag? And why? To keep an eye on me? A once-a-month checkup that I was doing okay? That I was happy?

Or was his motive more sinister? I needed the show to be over with, needed to sit him down and confront him. The Queen of Hearts always vanished right after her numbers. Not tonight, I vowed. I was going to stop her leaving if I had to tackle her to the ground and rip her wig off.

Everyone was on their feet applauding and I realized the show was done. I jumped up, clapping, as she took her curtsey center stage, and when she came up from it, I saw her glance at me, just a fast one, but slow enough that I caught it. "Jesse! I need to talk to her. Help me!"

Jesse nodded. The Queen disappeared behind her curtain and the Hatter killed the show lights, replacing them with lasers cutting through the sudden fog, as the light trance music became his normal hard house. People rushed the stage to dance, but I rushed to the curtain, Jesse behind me, Colton behind him.

I pulled back the curtain, just in time to see her disappear into the changing room, where queens and strippers and go-go boys waited for their moment onstage. "We'll wait for her right here!" I said.

"We can't. There's a back door to the room that leads to the storage at the rear, and then out into the alley. That's how she arrives without anyone seeing her," Jesse explained.

"Shit!" I did an about-face. "You guys wait here, I'm going out and around."

As I ran across the dance floor and up the stairs, my phone vibrated. "What?" I answered.

"So you see."

"Look, what's your game? Let me talk to Steven."

"Steven? You're running after Aaron. Which one do you want?"

"Fuck you!" I threw my phone to the ground as I hit the doors and went running around the building, past the stoners smoking up in the alley, past the entrance to the baths. I rounded the corner just in time to see a rectangle of light open. The back door to the club! And there she came out of it. The Queen of Hearts!

"Aaron!" I hollered. "Stop!"

I dodged the badly parked cars and grabbed his arm. He turned his face away from me. "Is it really you?"

He turned to look at me, tear-streaked mascara. I let him go. Slowly, he reached up and took off his wig, and there he was. How had I not recognized him? It was hidden under makeup but I knew that face. He reached out to touch me with a gloved hand.

"I didn't want you to know."

"What? What does this even mean?"

"Come with me to my place, and I'll tell you all about it. Don't hate me."

"I don't. I'm just so confused. What . . . ? When . . . ? Why . . . ?" Too many questions were filling my head. Where did I even start? "Shit, my phone. Can you wait?"

"Yes."

"Do you promise you'll wait?"

"It's out now. I don't have anything else to hide."

I ran back to the front door, and grabbed my phone, thanking God it was still there with so many people flooding past for the post-show cigarette. One of them was Twitten. "Tell Dinah and the others I'll call. I have to go." He barely had time to nod as I took off back around the building. I knew I'd get there only to find Aaron had left and I was already swearing at him in my head when I saw him still waiting for me in his gown, wig back on, leaning against his car.

"Get in. I'll tell you all about it."

Chapter 48

We didn't talk as he drove. I was in shock. What did this mean? Aaron had kicked his heels off and slid on runners when we got into the car. He navigated through the city streets, finally pulling up to an apartment building. One that was just a block away from the hotel he clearly had never been staying at. He parked in a stall out back.

"This is it," he said.

I didn't say anything as we got out of the car. With his heels and suitcase in hand, he took me up a couple flights of stairs ("Sorry, the elevator is out of order," he said) to a small bachelor suite. I knew the furniture. It all used to be mine. Ours.

"So you're just all settled in, eh?"

He had the decency to look ashamed. "I'm going to scrub out. Make yourself at home."

"Should be pretty easy, since all this was my home." It was all I could do to hold in the anger.

"There's gin on the counter, if you want to make us a couple drinks."

"This isn't a social call, Aaron."

"It might make it easier."

"It might at that." He went into the bathroom and I went to the kitchen, pouring us both very generous gin and crans. I knocked on the bathroom door.

"It's open."

Inside, he had stripped out of his outfit, and was bent over the sink. He was wearing just a black dance belt over pantyhose. His wig was on a dummy head on the countertop. Mussed boy hair, drag makeup, his smooth masculine torso, and then sleek pantyhose. I put the drink down and turned around. The visual was too disturbing. I left the door open though, and sat down on the couch. I could hear the water run as he began to scrub his face.

"Well?"

"Where do you want me to start?"

"Do you have Steven?"

"What? Don't be crazy, Alex."

"Says the guy who quit his job to become a drag queen stalker."

"When you left," he said, "I couldn't stop thinking about you. What you were doing. If you'd found a happiness that you never found when we were together. It consumed me."

"Did you try asking?"

"How do you ask that? How do you believe an answer? We tried to be friends, that first while, remember? But we fell out of touch, and I couldn't stand to see your Facebook posts about your new life. That's why I cut off all ties. I thought it would help me move on."

"Clearly, it didn't work."

"Clearly."

"So how did you end up here, like that?"

"I saw a posting on some gay site, Wonderland looking for a new entertainer, and at first, it was just some impossible idea. I thought I could come up, and be this big star, and show you how exciting life could still be. And then I thought, why not? So I applied."

"You'd never done drag before. How did you do it?"

"A lot of practice. Some online tutorials. Some pointers from queens at the bar back home."

"And then?"

"Wonderland loved me."

"So you quit your job and came here?"

"So I quit my job and came here. I had a pretty decent amount saved. You know how I am with money. I found this place on Craigslist and moved up, cutting off everyone back home. I went off the grid completely."

"But why?"

"I wanted to see you."

"I never went out those first couple years. How did you know I would end up at Wonderland?"

"I didn't know. I hoped. It sounds dumb, but I trusted in fate."

"You're right. It does sound dumb."

"But then my very first show as their new star entertainer, and there you were, in the front row, with your new boyfriend. It broke my heart, to see you so happy, and so in love."

"Why didn't you leave?"

"I'd signed a contract. And besides, I'd cut off my old life. If you could make it big and happy here, so could I."

"What have you been doing outside of drag?"

"I work part-time at this bookstore down the block. It keeps me busy."

"What if I'd gone in and seen you?"

"Because you suddenly read?"

He had me there, I hadn't read a book for fun since junior high. "So you've just spent the last six months like this?"

"Yes. And once a month, I would see you, with Dinah and your new friends, and your new boyfriend, and you were still so beautiful. Are still so beautiful. It made me happy to see you happy, made me feel like I was still a part of your life."

"That's crazy, Aaron."

"I know." He stood there, in the bathroom doorway, his face red from scrubbing, a towel around his waist, drink in hand. All traces of drag were gone, and it was just Aaron. "So what happens now?"

Chapter 49

I looked at him. It was just Aaron, but . . . it was Aaron. Six years, I thought. If it had been reversed, if Aaron had been the one to leave me, would I have just given up and accepted it? I couldn't know. I wouldn't have turned into a big drag queen though. How could Aaron's so familiar good looks have been so completely hidden by the Queen of Hearts's breathtaking beauty?

Or had I known all along? Was that why I'd always been so fixated on her?

"Alex, say something." He sat down on the arm of his chair, where he always used to sit and read the paper after work.

"Close your legs, I can see your dick."

He blushed and jumped to his feet. "I'll put on pants."

"Good idea."

I tried not to look as he changed, but I couldn't help it. As he bent over to pull on a pair of jeans, I smiled, seeing the dimple above his butt. "Commando, eh? I thought you didn't do that."

He turned around as he did up his pants. "Hush you. So . . ."

"What do you want me to say? It's almost unbelievable. That you've been here all this time?" He sat down next to me on the couch and I was all too aware of his shirtlessness. Was there still a hint of lip liner on his face because his mouth was . . . I leaned over and kissed him. I could feel his body shudder as he pulled away.

"So you're not mad?"

"Mad? I'm beyond mad, I don't even know what to say."

"Then why . . ."

"Don't overanalyze it. You always overanalyze it."

"Look who's talking."

"Hush you. But okay, wait a second, if you don't have Steven, who does?"

"I have no idea but do you really think I could do that to you? Not to mention kidnap and torture another human being?"

"No, but . . ."

"But what?"

"When I heard you spray-painted my door . . ."

He grabbed my shoulders. "Alex. I would never do that. I know how much you hate that word. I would never call you that."

"Well, my neighbor saw you."

"Did he? The neighbor you hate?"

"Well, we've kinda made peace."

"I think we should go see this good friend of yours and find out what the hell is going on."

"You swear you didn't."

"Alex, I swear. The first time I was ever in your building was when I was with you. I didn't even know what apartment was yours."

I raised an eyebrow. "You said that weird."

Aaron looked away. "Well, I knew where you lived. I might have followed you home after a show one night."

"Crazy!"

"Didn't you meet Steven by backing into his car?"

"That's different! I . . ."

"How is it different?"

"Well . . ." I couldn't come up with an argument to that one. "Let's go then."

Aaron finished getting dressed and then we drove first to the club, where Brandon told us the gang had already gone home, and then he offered us a drink. I was feeling the effects of the super-sized gin and cran I'd just had at Aaron's, though, and more alcohol was, for once, the last thing on my mind. As we got back into Aaron's car, I said, "I'd give you directions, but you clearly don't need them."

"Alex . . ."

"I think I'm entitled."

"Maybe a little."

"Crazy!"

"Hush you."

We pulled up outside of my building, and as Aaron got out of the car, I froze. "What's wrong?" he asked.

"He hasn't called back."

"Who?"

"Whoever has Steven. He knew I would see you, and he hasn't called back. I thought that something would happen tonight that would get Steven back, but . . ."

"Well, let's go up and talk to this Walrus. Maybe he knows more than he said."

"Maybe."

We got out of the car, entered the lobby, entered the elevator. As it went up, Aaron repeated, "I would never call you that."

"I know," I said.

"Just checking."

The door opened on my floor and standing there waiting for the elevator was Allan.

Chapter 50

"What are you doing here?" I said, getting off.

"Came to check on you, is all. You left so quick."

"Uhm, thanks? How do you even know where I live?"

"I came back with Walter. We were just worried. Look, I gotta go. Brandon's expecting me."

"Okay, sure." The doors closed behind him.

"That was strange," Aaron said.

"Very strange. I mean, I do not get this kid. He's friendly then psychotic, then best friends again."

"Drugs?"

"Definitely."

"Speaking of which, I don't approve."

"Hush."

"No, no hush. You're too smart for that shit, Alex. I thought you gave all that up when we started dating."

"I know. I did. I'm done with them. Again. Promise."

"Don't promise. Just do."

"Okay, okay, okay." I knocked on Walter's door.

"Who is it?"

"Alex. From across the hall."

"One second."

The door opened. He just stuck his face in the crack, not even taking the chain off. "What's up?"

"Walter, this is Aaron. Aaron, this is my neighbor Walter."

"Nice to meet you." Walter stuck his hand out and they shook. "Is that all?"

"But you've met before, right?"

"No, I don't think we have."

"But you've seen him?"

"Maybe, I don't know. Look, I have to go."

He went to shut the door and I jammed my foot in. "Your porn can wait. Open this door right now." Frowning, he undid the chain and I forced the door open. We stepped inside. "You know him, right?"

"Uhm . . ."

"Look, Walrus, I'm not kidding around here. Have you seen Aaron before?"

"I don't think so . . ."

"But didn't you tell me you saw me with him here the other night? Didn't you tell me you saw him spray-paint my door?"

"That," Aaron said, "is what's known as a leading question."

"Yes! I saw him. I . . ."

"You're lying," I said. "You lied about the whole thing. You never saw him do anything, you never even saw me with him. What the hell is going on, Walter?"

He sat down on the couch and started to cry. "I didn't want to lie to you. Not once I realized you were actually going to try to make amends. I didn't know what he was going to do when I buzzed him in, and then, he said that if I told you it was this guy here, if I said I saw him do it, he said . . ."

"Said what? Who said what?"

"He'd let me blow him. And he's so pretty, and I've . . . I've never done anything with a guy before, and it seemed like such a small thing. When he showed me his dick, and it was so big and hard, I couldn't say no." He was sobbing, and I was more than a little disgusted, and even though I was pretty sure who he was talking about, I needed him to say it.

"Who?"

"That guy Allan."

"That fucking psychopath! I'll kill him!"

"Now, calm down, Alex." Aaron put his hand on my shoulder but I just shook it off. I should've known he was involved in this, the way he'd come out of nowhere and the way he kept shifting mental gears between sane and a total lunatic.

"Why, Walter? Were you that hard up for dick? You had me convinced that Aaron was . . . that he had . . . I don't even have words. You're pathetic!" Walter was sobbing, and Aaron grabbed me.

"Alex, calm down, look at him, he's a mess. It was wrong but look at him." Aaron held my face locked toward Walter, crying on the couch. There was nothing at all attractive about him. I was physically repulsed. I wanted to shake him, strangle him! He looked up at me, all teary-eyed and snotty-nosed and . . . The only time I'd ever seen anyone cry that hard was Taylor, the night he . . . No! I wouldn't allow myself to compare this sad excuse for a human being to that beautiful boy. . . .

But they were the same. Sure, Taylor had been so amazing and I loved him so much, but inside, he was broken and lonely, and this guy here, whom I'd called Walrus the whole time I'd lived across the hall, was just as broken and just as lonely, and he hadn't ever loved anyone like I had loved Taylor, Aaron, Steven . . . He was alone.

"Fuck!" I swore, frustrated that I couldn't blame him. "Why, Walter? Did he say why he was doing this to me?"

"No, I swear, he just . . . Alex, I'm so sorry. Aaron, you too, I . . ."

"Where was he going?"

"Home I think. He didn't say. What are you going to do?"

"I'm going to hunt him down and string him up by his balls! That kid has a lot to answer for. C'mon, Aaron!" I grabbed his hand and led him out of the apartment, ignoring the sounds of Walter sobbing inside as I slammed the door.

Chapter 51

"Alex, you need to breathe! What are you going to do?"

"I'm going to find myself a twink and see what I can't shake out of him."

"Where? Where are you even going to go?"

"Back to Wonderland. If he's not there, Brandon will know where he is." I pushed the button for the elevator, again and again and again.

"It's sad, really," Aaron said.

"What? What's sad?"

"That guy back there. So desperate for human contact."

"Well, you go contact with him then. I'm furious."

"No, I get that. I just understand what it's like."

"Shut up, Aaron. I don't want to feel sorry for him right now. I'm sure tomorrow I will, but right now, I'm so mad. He made me believe that you . . . Ack! I don't even have words right now. Where the fuck is this elevator?"

Aaron laughed. "It's coming. Chillax."

"Chillax? Really? Are you twelve?" The elevator finally showed. I pushed him in, playfully for the most part. "Take me to the bar."

"Aye aye, boss!" He mock saluted me.

After we were in the car, he asked, "What are you going to do if he's there? You're not going to cause a scene right there?"

"I might. Look, you should be pissed too," I said. "He knocked you over."

"By accident."

"Oh? Are you sure? When he knocked you over, that's how I found out it was you, plus he's the one who framed you for painting my door."

Aaron drove in silence for a while. "Okay, why am I defending this little twink again?"

"Because you're a nice guy, but you shouldn't be."

"No, I shouldn't be." When we pulled up in front of the club, I told him to wait for me. "Nuh-uh," he said. "This is about me, too. I'm going to hold him down for you while we get some answers."

"That's the Aaron I know," I said with a grin. "You know, if you'd been willing to go to the bar and hold down a twink for me while I had my way with him before, we might still be together."

"Hush you." He paused, and frowned. "That wasn't funny."

"Too far, I admit. Sorry. After you?" I held the door open for him.

The night was winding down, and the crowd was a lot thinner than it had been even just half an hour ago. We looked around, but there was no sign of Allan anywhere in the bar. Cursing, I went up to the bar and waited for Brandon.

"Back already?" he said. "Just in time for last call."

"We're good," I said.

"We'll have a couple gin and crans," Aaron corrected. "Make them doubles."

While Brandon was pouring, I said, "I really don't need any more."

"Oh, I think we do."

Brandon brought over the drinks. "Where's Allan?" I asked.

"Why?"

"Just tell me where he is."

"I don't know and I don't care."

"Why? What's going on?"

"He's a loser. Let me just finish up here and I'll come tell you."

He went back to serving the last of his last call lineup. Aaron and I sat there at the bar, waiting. I must have been staring as per usual because Aaron turned to me and said, "Yes, it's a nice ass."

"I'm allowed to look."

"And drool?"

"I wasn't drooling."

"Not much anyway."

"Hush you."

My phone vibrated in my pocket. I had completely forgotten to be checking it. Seeing it was unknown, I ran to the bathroom so I could hear better as I answered. "Hello!"

"Where are you?"

"No, where are you? I want to talk to Steven, now!"

"You can talk to Steven tomorrow."

"No! No more tomorrows! We are ending this tonight!"

"Aren't you too busy drinking with your ex to worry about what I'm doing to poor little Stevie?"

"Look, I know who you are now, Allan, so I will be going to the cops. Put Steven on the phone so I can tell him I am on my way."

"Who's Allan? Some other trick of yours, you little faggot whore?"

"Faggot whore, eh? Dead giveaway. Pretty stupid, Allan, to call me what you wrote on my door."

"Whatever you're talking about doesn't matter. What matters is that you listen to me."

"No! You listen to me, you little fuckwad. When I get my hands on you . . ."

"Violence won't get you anywhere." And he hung up.

I kicked the counter, and flinched at the sudden sharp pain in my foot. Was it Allan? It didn't sound like him, come to think of it, although the way his fake accent kept changing, it was really impossible to tell.

All I could hope was that Brandon could tell me where I could find him.

Chapter 52

Back out at the bar, Brandon was just finishing off last call. He'd no sooner served his final customer than he stashed his tip jar under the counter, turned off the register, and came over. "Let's go outside. I need a smoke."

We followed him outside. "Why are you looking for Allan?"

"He's been fucking with me," I said.

"With us," Aaron corrected.

"You're not even going to believe me."

"Oh try me. I've been paying for his shit all week because he 'lost his wallet' last weekend, but he had it tonight when he was visiting the Caterpillar."

"Who's the Caterpillar?" Aaron asked.

"You've been performing here this long and don't know who the resident drug dealer is?"

"I don't do drugs."

"Still."

"Whoa," Brandon said. "Performing here?"

"Yeah, apparently my ex here decided to pursue his inner tranny and become the Queen of Hearts."

"Wow, you're amazing," Brandon said, bowing slightly.

"Enough of that! What about Allan's wallet?"

"Well, it's just symptomatic, isn't it? Says he doesn't have money because he lost his wallet, so I pay for drinks, dinners, whatever, but he pulls out his wallet tonight to get his crystal fix."

"The wallet at Steven's!" I said. "That fucking kid!"

"What?" they both said.

"I found a wallet at Steven's the other day, but thought it was his. And then when Aaron didn't have his yesterday—"

"—you naturally thought it was mine."

"Well, only because I believed the Walrus's story."

"Well, did you go check it?"

"I tried, but the house was trashed, and it was gone."

"But what does Allan have to do with Steven?" Brandon asked.

"I don't know, but if it was his wallet at Steven's house, then maybe he's the one who kidnapped him."

"He's a bit small to kidnap anyone, really," Aaron said. "Especially a built guy like Steven."

"Oh, I'm glad you noticed," I said.

"I had to check out the competition."

"I'm still confused," Brandon said.

"But pretty," I said, with a smile, and Aaron nodded his agreement. "Look, Allan persuaded the Walrus to let him into the building to graffiti my door, and then got him to lie and say he'd seen Aaron doing it."

"Persuaded how?"

"With his dick apparently."

"Oh he does have a beautiful dick, I'll give him that."

"I don't care how hung this kid is, I just want to see him hung by his balls."

"So you said," Aaron said.

"Where does he live, Brandon?"

"No idea, we always went to my place."

"Well, call him. Get him here."

Brandon pulled his phone out of his sock and called. "There's no answer."

"Fuck, now what?"

"Where did you meet him anyway?"

"He came up to me at the bar."

"Just some random?"

"Don't judge me," Brandon said. "You're no saint."

"That's not what I meant, Brandon. I just mean, maybe it was planned."

"Planned? Maybe you're paranoid and he just wanted my ass. Everyone wants my ass."

"Who can blame them?" Aaron said.

Brandon grinned. "Oh yeah? Well, we can definitely talk about that."

I was both annoyed and jealous. "If you two don't mind."

"Sorry, where was I?" Brandon said. "Oh yeah, look, I know you're going through a lot with Steven right now, but I really don't think Allan is smart enough to pull it off."

He had me there. "Look, I just want to find out if he knows anything. Any idea where he could be?"

"No clue. He was going to meet me after work though, so he should be along shortly."

I wasn't so sure. If he suspected I was onto him, and thought I was at the club, he'd avoid it. I pointed that out, and Aaron, right as always, pointed out that I didn't really have much of a choice.

We had to wait.

Chapter 53

The bar closed, with no sign of Allan, surprise surprise, and, surprise surprise, he didn't answer when Brandon called. We stuck around as Brandon and the rest of the staff closed up, hoping Allan would call. Once the door was locked, the Hatter joined everyone at the bar, and slammed down a bottle of Patron.

"Shots for everyone."

"I'm good," I said.

"If you're staying, you're drinking. You too, Queen," he said to Aaron.

"How did you know?"

"I'm the Hatter," he said simply, pouring out shots. "Cheers!" We all raised our glasses, and tipped them back.

"I need a chaser," I gagged, and Brandon slid down his beer, grabbing another from the cooler.

"I'll have one too," Aaron said, "since we're drinking more."

I should have stopped it right there. It was a feeling in the pit of my stomach, sickening and inevitable. We had a couple beers while Brandon cashed out, and then he tried to call Allan again, and there was still no answer. We gave up for the night; what choice was there?

We walked Brandon home, as he drunkenly and dramatically cried about yet another failed relationship. Neither of us had the heart to tell him that seven days hardly constituted a relationship. We talked about it after Brandon went up to his apartment, just there in the street, and then Aaron asked, "Did you want to come over?"

My head was light, and my heart was heavy, and my body was tired. His place was so close. "I don't think that's a good idea."

"No sex, I promise."

"Oh, I'm so drunk that wouldn't be an issue."

"That's never stopped you before." He grinned.

"Hush you."

"Come over."

"Maybe for a while."

We didn't say much as we walked, and we didn't really say anything when we got to his apartment. He poured us nightcaps, and we sat there on the couch, and just sipped them.

"Aaron," I said suddenly, just as he said, "Look, Alex, I know you've got a lot going on right now, and this is completely bad timing but—"

"Don't," I said. "Just don't." I looked at him, knowing what he wanted to say, and part of me wanted to at least hear him say it. We sipped our drinks. I got up and looked out the window. "Not much of a view," I said, looking out onto the parking lot.

"It was never a long-term place."

"What was it, Aaron? Did you really think this was the way to get me back?"

"I wasn't thinking. I just wasn't ready to completely say good-bye."

"But we had said good-bye. It was done."

"Is it still?" He wrapped his arms around me from behind. I felt myself tense, and then I relaxed back into his arms, my head on his shoulder.

"Yes."

"Oh."

"I bought a ring."

"What?"

"For Steven. I was going to ask him to marry me. That's why I freaked out and went out and got high. That's why he found drugs on me, and broke up with me. And then he went missing."

Aaron let out a huge breath, and then let go of me. "Why would you tell me that?"

"You needed to know."

"You're here in my apartment, and we've spent all this time together, including fucking twice, and of course I'm going to start feeling all these old feelings. And then you stand there, while I'm holding you, and you tell me you were going to propose?" His eyes were teary. "Why did I need to know?"

"So you don't think this means more than it does," I said, and I kissed him. He shuddered and shook and then was kissing me back. I don't know how long that kiss lasted, but I pulled away eventually. "Let's go to bed," I said, grabbing his hand.

Chapter 54

I woke up before Aaron did and crawled out of bed slowly. He was sleeping there so peacefully, in our bed. I didn't want to wake him. We'd had our moment, and it was done. Now I had to find Allan and, hopefully, Steven. I got dressed as quietly as possible, and then I slipped out.

As I headed down the elevator, I thought that maybe I should have left a note or something. But a note implied more than I wanted it to be. It had been wrong, but it was a good-bye. What was that Bette Midler movie, where sometimes you needed to get it out of your system, one last time scratching an itch? That's all it had been.

Which didn't stop Aaron from texting me before I'd even flagged a cab outside. **You could've woken me.**

Sorry, you were sound asleep.

What more could I say? In a way, he had done something grand and romantic and brave, the kind of crazy that our relationship had lacked there at the end. In another way though, he had done something completely insane, the kind of crazy that I couldn't just overlook. And even if I was able to, I had other more pressing crazy to deal with: Allan.

I texted Brandon, knowing he'd still be asleep but wanting to remind him to call me as soon as he got up. I sent out a mass text to Dinah and the twins letting them know that everything was good, or at least, that nothing had changed.

The cab dropped me off at my place, and I hopped out. When I got up to my apartment, there was a note taped to the door. "Sorry sorry sorry sorry," it read, "I hope you can forgive me." I glared at Walter's door, sure I would forgive him eventually but not in the mood to do so yet. All the time I'd wasted thinking it was Aaron behind everything, when really, it was that tweaked-out little twinkie I should have suspected right from the moment he pinned me against the wall at White Night.

Griffin was happy to see me, and I gave him a good scratching and some food as I figured out my next move. There wasn't much I could do really, other than wait, but I decided to go to Steven's and at least finish cleaning it up, and feed his fish. Did that make up for leaving him in the hands of a crazy person for a week? Did it make up for spending a night having what had been truly amazing and passionate sex with my ex? No, but it was a start.

The late September air was brisk as I walked to Steven's, ignoring the crowds of Saturday morning shoppers clogging up the downtown streets. I was all too aware of my phone not vibrating in my pants pocket, even as I was all too aware of the ring box, bulky and uncomfortable and pressing against my hip in the other pocket. I still wanted to marry him. All the drunken sexcapades of the week aside, Aaron being in town aside, I wanted Steven.

As I turned onto his block, I paused, and then did a quick about-face. There were two police cars outside of the house. I'd forgotten about them completely. I had myself so convinced to not go to them for help as per my orders from Allan or whoever it was. They hadn't been at the club last night, and that's where I'd told them Steven was meeting me. What were they thinking now that he hadn't contacted them yet? Was I considered a suspect in some unspecified crime?

I popped into a Starbucks about a block away and grabbed myself a Pumpkin Spice Latte. I sat at the window and watched the people go by, like Steven and I used to do on those rare chilly summer nights. What was he doing right now? Was he tied to a chair, crying and bleeding? Was he blindfolded? I could picture the bruises on his handsome face.

That's it, I decided, *I'm going to talk to those officers. They'll find him for me, and then I can kiss away the bruises, both the ones on his skin, and the ones on his heart from everything I've done.*

I was almost back at Steven's when my phone rang. It was Brandon. "Allan wants to meet me at my place. Want to come over and talk to him?"

"Yes. Yes I do." I did an about-face again and headed toward Brandon's. The thought of pinning Allan up against the wall and getting some answers out of him made me smile hard for the first time in a long time. "When is he getting there?"

"Not for an hour."

"I can be there in about fifteen. You're going to have to be nice."

"Why? I'm pissed at him."

"I want him comfortable and relaxed. He might be paranoid and jumpy so this is it, I'll wait until he's completely complacent, and then *BAM!* Twink goes down."

I got to Brandon's and we talked for a while, waiting for Allan to buzz. As soon as he did, I hid in the closet, something I hadn't done in nearly fifteen years, I noted with a smile. It was a bit trite, maybe, hiding and then springing out in some big AHA moment, but a lot of this had been pretty B-movie drama anyway, so what was one more time?

Through the slightly open door, I could see Brandon pace, and the look on his face was still pretty annoyed. *He better pull himself together,* I thought. There was a knock on the door, and Brandon opened it. Allan flew into his arms and it was all I could do not to fly out at him right then. Somehow I restrained myself.

"Why didn't you come back last night?" Brandon asked, and I gritted my teeth. He was going to blow it.

"Sorry, I ran into some friends and we ended up partying till like seven this morning. I missed you though."

Before I knew what was happening, Allan was stripping off his pants. Brandon looked askance in my direction, unsure what to do. I wasn't sure what to do either, but his dick was very impressive like I'd heard. Who'd've thought a twink that small would be hung like that? I couldn't help but watch as he started kissing Brandon hard, his hand inside the back of Brandon's jeans. He pushed Brandon down on the couch and was standing above him. His dick was even more impressive fully erect, and the thought of that massive dick plowing into Brandon's beautiful ass was more than enough to make me hard.

Before I got completely distracted, I threw the door open. Allan screamed, "What the fuck?" and started scrambling for his pants. I stepped in front of the door, cutting off his escape. "What the hell,

Brandon? Alex, what are you doing here?" He pulled his pants on, and I couldn't help but be a little disappointed.

"If this is a threeway, I'm really not down for that."

"Oh there's not going to be any threeway, kid. I want some answers."

"Get the fuck out of my way. I'm leaving," he said, and tried to push past me.

I held my ground. "You're not going anywhere, Allan. Not until you tell me everything you know about where Steven is."

He grinned at me.

Chapter 55

"I don't know what you're talking about." I wanted to smack the smug grin off his face.

"Walter told me everything. He told me you painted my door, he told me you got him to lie about Aaron."

"And let him suck your dick for it!" Brandon yelled, jumping on Allan and pummelling him with his fists.

Allan screamed out, and as much as I didn't care, I pulled Brandon off. Allan lay there on the floor, shaking. Brandon was vibrating and panting. "Stop it!" I told him. "I need answers and that's not helping. You can pound on him later."

"Fuck you both," Allan said.

"Just tell me. What the fuck did I ever do to you?"

"I just did it for money! I got offered a thousand dollars to do it. Well, part of it was for that fat fuck, but why share my money when he was just as happy to suck my dick?"

"Don't you have any respect for yourself?" Brandon asked.

"Oh grow up. Why would I respect myself? We're just fags."

"How did you get so twisted so young?" I asked. "No, never mind. I don't even care. Where's Steven?"

"I don't know. I never met him."

"You're lying. You left your wallet at his house and then broke in to get it. Did you have to smash our pictures?"

"What? I never did that."

"Allan, don't fuck with me. Brandon told me you lost your wallet."

"Yeah, so what? When you've got a cock like mine, fags will pay for anything you need." He sneered at Brandon, who jumped on him again. This time, Allan was ready and got in a punch on Brandon's jaw.

"You fucking bastard! I liked you!"

"Brandon! Not now!" I hollered. "Allan, who paid you this money? And why?"

"Some guy, I don't know his name."

"Look," I said, getting to my knees, grabbing him by the collar and pulling him so close to me our noses were nearly touching. "Tell me everything you know right now or you're going to be very, very sorry." Allan bravely licked his lips and smirked. "I'm not fucking kidding, Allan. Start talking."

"Some guy came up to me at the bar last Friday and pointed you out."

"Who? What guy?"

"I'd never seen him before. Late twenties, tall, good-looking, but just a fag."

"What did he tell you?"

"He asked me if I wanted to make an easy grand, and I said of course. I figured he wanted to fuck me or something. Who doesn't want to get with me, really? But he said I just had to play a few little tricks. Nothing even that bad. Slip you some G, shit like that."

"G? When was that?"

"The other night in the club. When you went home for that four-some."

That didn't make it better, but it did explain it a bit more anyway. Why didn't that help with my guilt though? "Did he say why?"

"I didn't ask. He just told me where you lived and what to do."

"And just gave you the money?"

"No, only two hundred dollars. I didn't get the rest till last night. Fuck, we had a kiki."

"I don't care about your drug-fueled orgies. So you saw this guy again?"

"Yeah, a couple times."

"How does he get a hold of you?"

"I gave him my number."

"Do you have his?"

"No, it's blocked."

"And why me then? Was that why you came on to me?" Brandon asked, crying.

Allan shrugged. "You were a hot piece of ass, too, and it's always good to blow the bartender."

I raised my hand to preemptively hold Brandon off from giving the kid another well-deserved beating. "Is there anything else you're doing for him?"

"No, I'm off the hook, now free to enjoy my money. It was easy and it was fun."

"Was that why you were at White Night?"

"I was just supposed to make sure you hooked up. Sure didn't take you long either. For someone supposedly so in love."

"What do you know about love?" Brandon spat at him.

"Brandon, chill! Go calm down in the other room and leave me and Allan alone for a minute." Brandon went into the bedroom and slammed the door. "Okay, Allan, look, I don't give a shit what your problems are. You're clearly fucked up and you're going to have a miserable life. I just want to know how I can find this guy."

"You're out of luck, Alex. He met me at the bar last night, and the money went from him to me to the Caterpillar and I was off. All I had to do was make sure I knocked over that drag queen."

"He was at the club last night?"

"He was sitting right behind you."

"Who? What was his name at least?"

"His name was A Thousand Dollars. Who the fuck cared what his name was? It was cash. He was just some guy."

I looked him in his soulless blue eyes. I knew that was all I was going to get from him.

"Get out of here," I said, letting go of him.

Chapter 56

He was up and out fast, slamming the door behind him. Brandon came bounding out of the bedroom. "What the fuck? Why would you let him go?"

"Oh, shut up and calm down. We're following him."

I stuck my head into the hallway. Allan was waiting for the elevator. He didn't even think to glance back as he got in. "Come on," I said as soon as the door closed, and Brandon and I raced down the stairs to the lobby.

"What are we doing?" Brandon asked.

"I think he does know who this guy is, and I bet he gets in touch with him. If he got a thousand bucks out of him so easily, a user like that will want to keep him around."

The elevator stopped, and Allan got out. We watched from the stairwell. He was on his phone, and that was a good sign as far as I was concerned. Allan left the lobby and headed down the street.

"Quick. Let's go."

It was ridiculous to see, I'm sure, the way we followed Allan, leaping behind light posts, peering out from behind buildings. Brandon got caught up in it, and started acting even more obviously furtive, if that's even a thing. Allan didn't look back once. He was still on his phone. Who was he talking to? Where was he going?

Eventually, he reached an apartment building and we watched from across the street as he spoke on the intercom and then was buzzed in. As soon as he was out of sight, we ran up but the directory was only numbers, no names.

"What now?" Brandon asked.

"I guess we wait," I said. "I doubt Allan will answer your calls at this point."

"Who do you think he's talking to? The guy who paid him?"

"That's what I'm hoping. It's my only hope right now." There was a Starbucks across the street, and Brandon and I went and got coffee, never taking our eyes off the front door of the building.

We'd no sooner sat down than my phone rang. It was, unsurprisingly, the dreaded unknown number. "What?" I said into the phone.

"You're being a little aggressive, don't you think?"

"Because we roughed up your twink? It's going to get a lot worse for you when I find out who you are. Just tell me this, why me and Steven?"

"Proof."

"Proof of what?"

"Proof that you fags are twisted and don't even know what real love is. You say you're the same as everyone else, but you're not. You're depraved and perverted."

"Look who's talking! Look at what you've done, what you're doing."

"Do you want to talk to your boyfriend, Alex? Do you want to tell him everything you've done?"

"Yes, I want to talk to him."

"Well, you can't. You can sit there, sipping your coffee, and you can think you're in love, but I know the truth." He could see us, I realized! As I listened to his ranting, I scanned the building across the way, and sure enough, I could see, in a window on the third floor, a shadow standing there. "I know how sick you really are."

"What do you want? Do you want me to agree with you? Do you want me to tell you that yes, I'm human, I made mistakes? Yes, I'm a man, sometimes I think with my dick and do things I regret? I've done drugs when I knew it was stupid, I've sucked dick when I knew it was wrong? That doesn't change anything about how I feel about Steven."

"How you feel about Steven . . . oh yes, Alex, talk about your feelings, like a fucking sissy. You make me sick."

"I want to talk to Steven. Let me talk to Steven."

"I want to talk to Steven. Let me talk to Steven." In his mimicking tone, for a second, I almost recognized the voice.

"Goddammit! What do I have to do to end this already? White Night, the show, I don't get what you're after."

"You will." He laughed. "Oh you will." He hung up.

"Fuck!" I said, slamming my phone down.

"What?" Brandon asked. "What does he want?"

"I don't know. I have no fucking clue!"

"Look!" Brandon said, pointing across the street. Someone was holding the door of the building open as an old woman unloaded groceries from a cab and took them into the lobby.

"Quick!" I said. "Before that door closes."

We ran across the street and through the open door. I raced up the stairs to the third floor. It had been on the street side, two in from the corner. Was that him? Was that where he was? Was Steven there?

"Wait, wait," Brandon said, panting behind me. "What are you going to do? You can't just smash a door down."

"Like hell I can't," I said, and threw myself at the apartment door.

Chapter 57

"Ow! Fuck!" I said, lying there on the hallway floor.

"Like I said, you can't. You're mad, but you're not that strong." Brandon offered his hand to help me up.

The door opened. An old man stood there in the doorway. "What's going on out here?"

"Let me talk to Steven!" I said, scrambling to my feet and pushing myself into his apartment.

"Here now! What's your issue?" he said, stepping in front of me.

"Steven!" I called. "Steven!"

"Alex, come here!" Brandon yelled from the hall.

"Fuck!" I heard someone else yell. It was Allan's voice. "Sorry!" I apologized to the man as I ran back into the hall. Allan was running down the stairs. "Where did he come from?" I asked Brandon.

"There!" he said, pointing at the next door over.

"Open up!" I yelled, banging on the door. "Open this fucking door!"

"You kids, I'm calling the cops if you don't clear out."

"Shut up!" I screamed at the old man. "Open up! Brandon, go grab Allan."

"Why . . ."

"Just do it, and get him back here." I slammed into the door with my shoulder. "Open up!" Brandon took off after Allan down the stairs. The neighbor had retreated back inside. Part of me hoped he was calling the police. They'd get me in. "Open up! Steven!"

The door opened. "Alex, hello." He was familiar, but I didn't know him.

"Who are you?"

"It's been a while," he said, "but I'm surprised you don't recognize me."

"Should I?"

"We went to school together for ten years."

The man's face wandered through my mind in search of a memory. It came to me, the picture of two kids and a computer screen filled with tits. "Nathan?"

"Well done, Alex. You might as well come in." He pushed the door open the whole way, and there, in the middle of the room, was Steven, tied to a chair, his eye bruised, his lip bleeding. It was my worst nightmare, and this time, I wasn't waking up.

"Steven!" I ran to him. "Oh my God, my God, my God. Are you okay?" I pulled the gag out of his mouth, my eyes stinging with hot tears. I touched his face, and he flinched.

"Alex, thank God, thank God, thank God."

I kissed his lips, tentatively.

"Now, now, none of that sick faggot shit."

I spun around. Nathan was locking the door, pulling the chain across it. "What a touching reunion. Who'd have thought that you'd be so happy to see each other when you just spent the night with your ex?"

I lurched to my feet. "What the fuck? Why?"

"Because you're sick, Alex. I've known it since school. When you tried to touch me. You're wrong. And it's spreading."

"What is?"

"Your sickness. Your disgusting faggotry. It's everywhere. It didn't used to be, but now it is, and people think it's okay, people think it's normal, people think you're just born like that. I know better! I know how wrong it is. Look how easy it was to get you to betray someone you say you love. You don't know love. You're twisted. Twisted!"

"Nathan, it *is* normal! You *are* born that way. Look, it's—"

"Shut your lying mouth! It's wrong!"

"Let us go, Nathan. Let us go, and I won't say anything. Just let us go."

"I don't think so, Alex. It has to stop. The spread of the disease has to end now." He reached behind his back and pulled out a handgun. He raised it. "God wants me to stop it."

"Nathan, no!" I screamed, and jumped toward him. I knocked the gun from his hand, knocked him to the ground. We grappled. I was vaguely aware of Steven calling out for me. Nathan was stronger than me though, I could tell, and although I struggled against him, he pinned me to the ground, and slammed his fist into my face. Pain and fire shot through my head, and the room went dark.

Chapter 58

I opened my eyes. Well, eye. The other one felt swollen shut. Everything was a blur, but it slowly came back into focus. I was tied tightly to a chair, next to Steven. We'd been dragged from the living room into the bedroom, and were both gagged. Our chairs were right next to each other. I could see his beautiful and battered face. "I love you," I mumbled through the gag.

"How precious!" Nathan was sitting on the bed, watching us. He had the gun in his hand. "This is what passes for love now? Two men? It's foul." He got to his feet. "You were my friend. I trusted you. And then you tried to touch me. Like I was like you. Like I could ever be like you. I couldn't even look at you without seeing it inside you, like a demon trying to eat me. It had already eaten you.

"And then you met Taylor, and there were two of you. And you seemed so happy, but I knew you weren't. I knew it was all a lie. How could it bring happiness when it was wrong? You were both sick, but you didn't know it. Taylor did though. Taylor knew the only way to fix himself was to die."

I struggled against the ropes, screaming against the gag. I didn't want to hear this. I didn't want to hear him talking about Taylor. He was pacing, wild-eyed and waving the gun around.

"You know I'm right, Alex. You know how diseased you are. Steven knows. He was crying. Just walking and crying and he told me everything. It didn't take much either. A shoulder to cry on, that's all.

"I'd been watching you, you see. I saw you one day, and you looked so happy, and I knew it couldn't be true. So I started watching you. I was going to use you to prove to the world that you people aren't like everyone else. It's different. You say it's not a lifestyle but look at you: drugs and bars and baths, and all you care about is getting high and getting off.

"Even this one. Oh you should've heard all he said after I got him here, got him tied up. He said he loved you, that he wanted to spend his whole life with you. That's easy enough, neither of you have much time left. But no matter what lies came out of his mouth, it didn't take him long to invite me to his place. Oh sure, he said it was just to talk, but all I had to do was kiss him, and he melted.

"What? Don't look at me like that. I had to do it. It was for a greater good. I let him kiss me, and then invited him over. And then *BAM!*" He smacked me across the face. "Just like that I had him, had you. I was going to make him see that you're just a fag, just like him. You can't love.

"You must have loved it, eh? Being able to go out and get your rocks off, fucking some strange guy, and being able to blame it all on me. You're welcome for that. Allan was more than happy to help me, by keeping an eye on you, by helping me fuck with your head. All he cared about was getting money to get high. Just like the rest of you. Only caring about satisfying his urges.

"Well I have urges too!" He smacked me again, then smacked Steven. "I have the urge to wipe all of you off the face of the earth. You, this one, your ex . . ." He laughed. "Yes, that was just an extra perk. When I found out that the guy you hooked up with at the bathhouse—and really, what kind of normal people have a place just for fucking strangers; oh yeah, you're the same as us. When Allan overheard the two of you talking and I realized that you had banged your ex, oh, that was an even better opportunity. You were so committed to this one here, weren't you?" He grabbed my face, turned my head toward Steven. "Look at him. Tell him how many times you had sex this week! Oh, it was a lot more than the one I made you have, wasn't it?" He ripped my gag out. "Wasn't it?" he screamed. "Tell him!"

"Fuck you, Nathan!"

"Wrong answer!" He brought the butt of the gun down hard on my head. I saw spots.

There was a sudden banging on the door to the apartment. "Alex? Are you in there?" It was Brandon's voice.

Nathan shoved the gag back in my mouth and yanked it tight. "You shut your mouths. Both of you."

He left the room, and I looked at Steven. He was crying, and the cut on his forehead had opened back up. Blood was dripping down his face.

I could hear Nathan at the door. "Sorry, I don't know any Alex." I grunted, but it was futile. The gag was too tight.

"But he was here when I left. This is the apartment Allan left from."

"Oh Allan, yes, I know Allan." I jumped with my chair, closer to Steven.

"What was Allan doing here?"

I strained against the rope but, again, they were too tight. Steven shook his head at me, a resigned expression on his face.

"He sucks my dick for money."

"What?" Brandon screeched.

"Oh, didn't you know? He's a great little cocksucker."

I could hear Brandon scream as Nathan laughed and shut the door. He came back in. "Oh, you fags are so emotional. Your friend there, Brandon is it? He's known that druggie for a week and he's so upset. They don't even really know each other. I know that druggie loser better than he does. Cash and cock, that's all he cared about. Not that they're both not druggie losers. You all are. That's how it all started, didn't it? You going out and getting high."

He was pacing again as he talked, and stopped in front of Steven. "What do you think, Steven? Do you think your perfect little boyfriend is clean? We already know he was fucked up again this week. Do you think he's got more on him right now? Let's find out."

He took a step toward me and started going through my pockets. I tried to push him off, but couldn't. "Oh, what's this?" He pulled out the ring box. "Oh look, Stevie. Your little boyfriend was going to propose." He took the ring out of the box. "Isn't that fucking precious?" He sneered, and then *BAM!* He kicked me in the chest, almost knocking me over. "You sick twisted deviant! How dare you think you can get married? Two men? That's sick. It's wrong, wrong." He cradled his head in his hands and then let out a roar. "Let's see how it looks, shall we?" He jammed the ring onto Steven's finger. "Look at that. Isn't it wonderful?" He grabbed me by the hair and held my face up to the ring. "Do you Alex take this man?" He reared his head back and spat in my face. It was wet and thick, and I could feel it slowly dripping down my face.

I felt a vibration in my pocket. Nathan must have heard it. He grabbed my phone from my pocket. "Oh, it's just Brandon, looking for you no doubt. Stupid little faggot. Well let's make sure we don't have any more interruptions, okay?" He dropped my phone to the floor and smashed it with the heel of his foot. "Now, where were we?"

Chapter 59

He ripped the gag out of my mouth and said, "Now behave. No screaming, no fighting, just tell Steven that you're a disgusting creature."

"Fuck you!" I spat in his face.

He smacked me again. "Wrong answer. Tell your little boyfriend, oh sorry, fiancé now, tell him how sick you are. How much you loved all those drugs in your nose, all that dick up your ass."

"No."

He pointed the gun at Steven's head and cocked the hammer. "Tell him, or he dies now."

"Stop, please!" It didn't even sound like my voice. I was gasping for air, between the tears and the blows, and I just wanted it to stop. "I'll tell him anything you want. Just please, don't hurt him."

"You're not a man. You're weak and sad."

"Yes!"

"Why couldn't you have killed yourself like Taylor?"

Hearing his name again ripped the heart from my chest. "Stop saying his name!"

"Does that hurt you? That you were too much of a coward to do what he did? He knew he was a perversion. He knew what you two were doing was wrong."

"Shut up! He was perfect!"

"He was foul! And he is better off dead! You all would be better off dead, burning in hell where you belong!"

"Why, Nathan? Why do you hate us so much?"

"Because you're sick!" He was screaming, crying. "You're sick!"

"You're the sick one! What? Are you gay and just too much of a fucking coward to admit it? You kissed Steven. You let Allan suck your dick. Just be a fucking man and admit it."

"Shut up!" He knocked my chair over and straddled me, grabbing my shoulders and banging me against the floor. "Shut up! Shut up! You're the sick ones! You fuck anything! You don't know what love or trust is. All you care about is your dicks!"

"No, that's not true! We—"

"Shut up! It is true! You said you loved this one but you still stuck your dick in any guy that came along. When you were drunk or high. You think that makes it okay? That you can blame it on the drugs? Blame it on the beer? You can't! You have to accept the consequences for what you do! You can't just come into someone's room and touch them! You can't just make them do stuff to you and then apologize in the morning and say it won't happen again! And then it does happen again! You can't do that! It's your fault! It's your fault!" He kept banging the chair against the floor, and I felt the back of the chair break.

"Ah! You're sick!" He jumped to his feet and I could feel that my arms were looser. His banging had freed me. "You need to die!" He pointed the gun at me. "You both need to die! You can't do that to a little boy! It's your fault! It's your fau . . ." I jumped to my feet and tackled him. The gun went flying across the floor. I pulled my arms free as he jumped at me. I was barely aware of Steven struggling in his chair. Nathan was flailing madly, screaming insensibly. I dove for the gun. He grabbed my collar and pulled me back. We both hit the ground. He was on my back, holding me down, and then slammed my head against the floor.

The room spun. I bucked him off. The gun was ahead of me, on the floor, just out of reach. I jerked across the hardwood. "Fucking faggot!" Nathan screamed behind me. My fingers touched the gun, but then Nathan was on me. "You can't! You're sick! It's sick! It's sick!" I felt the handle of the gun in my hand. Nathan was screaming and I saw his fist coming toward my face and then *BANG!*

Chapter 60

I lay there, unable to move, barely able to breathe, and then I heard Steven screaming through his gag. I got to my knees. Nathan was on the floor. All I could see was blood. I could feel the vomit rising up inside me, but just when I thought I couldn't hold it back, I heard Steven again.

"Oh my God!" I crawled toward him. His eyes were wide and teary. I pulled the gag from his mouth and kissed his lips.

"Oh my God, thank God, oh Alex, Alex."

I untied him and he fell into my arms. "Steven, Steven, are you okay? I am so sorry you had to—"

"Don't say anything. I'm just glad it's over. I love you, Alex. I love you." He was covering my face in kisses.

His tears were hot on my fingers as I cradled his face next to mine. "Is he . . . ?" Steven crawled toward Nathan's body. "Don't touch him!" I couldn't think.

"He's breathing," Steven said.

"Let's just go! Let's leave!" I helped Steven to his feet and he wrapped his arm around me. "I love you, Steven. I love you." We fled the apartment, and Steven collapsed on the street outside.

Chapter 61

Saturday morning brunch at the Duchess was a tradition, and the boys were already there when we arrived. Jesse and Colton had brought along the boy they'd taken home from Wonderland the night before. He was a pretty little ginger kid, with a beard that seemed out of place on his baby face. They'd also brought along Walter, which I still had a problem with, but I was willing to overlook what he had done; God knows I had done enough things that were getting overlooked. Brandon was flying solo, having sworn off men in the week since he'd last seen Allan. Dinah and Christopher showed up just as we were sitting down, and there were hugs all around.

"I'd like to propose a toast," Jesse said, and we all lifted our mimosas. "Congratulations are definitely in order."

We clinked glasses around the table.

"Hey, did I miss a toast?" Aaron said, joining us.

"Sorry darling," Jesse said, "but we couldn't wait."

"Well, let me catch up." He grabbed a mimosa from a passing waiter and raised his glass. "I just wanted to thank you for inviting me. I know this isn't easy but—"

"Hey! None of that! This is a happy occasion," Colton said. "You're not the Queen of Hearts here, so sit down and shush." He stuck out his tongue, and we laughed.

As we sat down, Steven squeezed my hand under the table. It had been his idea to invite Aaron, and I might never understand why. He had insisted though, and I wasn't about to argue with him. I owed him too much for that.

We hadn't talked about what had happened the week he was taken. All he had said was that it didn't matter, that he was just glad to be back with me, and just wanted to put it all behind us. How we were going to do that with Aaron at the brunch table was beyond me, but with the ring on his finger, Steven got his wish.

Nathan had put the ring there, but when we were in bed at home that night, Steven asked me if I meant it. If I had really meant to propose. I said yes. He said yes. And there the ring was, and there it would stay, and as long as it stayed there, Steven could have anything he wanted.

Aaron and I, on the other hand, had talked. He said he understood. He said he knew what it was like, feeling that old feeling, and that he just wanted me to be happy. If Steven made me happy, then that made him happy, he said, and I assured him, Steven made me happy.

As we laughed and tried to make everything seem normal again, I thought about all the unanswered questions I had. Nathan had been unconscious when the police arrived, but since then, his condition had stabilized in the hospital. I wouldn't go see him, even if the police let me. Anything I needed to know would become clear during the trial. If there was a trial.

So he had been hurt as a kid. So what? Steven had heard all about it during his captivity. How his father had raped him. How his father's friends had raped him. How he had obsessed over me for years, making that innocent teenage touch into something so much more evil. Did it matter if he'd been hurt? Did that make everything he had done understandable? Maybe. Maybe not. Was he gay himself? Steven thought so. Did it matter? Maybe. Maybe not. I didn't hate him. He was another broken person. There were too many broken people in the world, and maybe he was more broken than most, but I couldn't fix anyone. Anyone except myself.

And there was a lot inside me I needed to fix. That was something I had learned though this ordeal. When Steven looked at me though, when his eyes lit up with such warmth and love, I knew I'd get there eventually. I squeezed his hand back and smiled.

Don't miss Alex's next adventure, *Through the Mirrorball*,
coming in May 2015!

About the Author

Rob Browatzke has been writing for as long as he can remember, and is pretty darn excited for someone else to be reading his stuff finally! When it comes to gay bars and booze and drugs and drama, he knows what he's talking about. He has over fifteen years of experience working in gay clubs in Edmonton, Alberta, and his current Wonder-lounge is every bit as amazing as Alex's Wonderland. Feel free to stalk him on Facebook and Twitter (@robbrowatzke).

Printed in the United States
by Baker & Taylor Publisher Services